Milk

by Emily DeVoti

A SAMUEL FRENCH ACTING EDITION

SAMUEL FRENCH

FOUNDED 1830

NEW YORK HOLLYWOOD LONDON TORONTO

SAMUELFRENCH.COM

MUSIC USE NOTE

Licensees are solely responsible for obtaining formal written permission from copyright owners to use copyrighted music in the performance of this play and are strongly cautioned to do so. If no such permission is obtained by the licensee, then the licensee must use only original music that the licensee owns and controls. Licensees are solely responsible and liable for all music clearances and shall indemnify the copyright owners of the play and their licensing agent, Samuel French, Inc., against any costs, expenses, losses and liabilities arising from the use of music by licensees.

IMPORTANT BILLING AND CREDIT
REQUIREMENTS

All producers of *MILK must* give credit to the Author of the Play in all programs distributed in connection with performances of the Play, and in all instances in which the title of the Play appears for the purposes of advertising, publicizing or otherwise exploiting the Play and/or a production. The name of the Author *must* appear on a separate line on which no other name appears, immediately following the title and *must* appear in size of type not less than fifty percent of the size of the title type.

In addition the following credit *must* be given in all programs and publicity information distributed in association with this piece:

Excerpts from the book *Keeping A Family Cow*, by Joann S. Grohman, used with permission of the author.

MILK was first produced by New Georges (Susan Bernfield, Artistic Director; Sarah Cameron Sunde, Associate Director) and New Feet Productions in New York City on April 29, 2010. The performance was directed by Jessica Bauman, with sets by Susan Zeeman Rogers, costumes by Emily Pepper, lighting by Lenore Doxsee, and sound by Amy Altadonna. The production stage manager was Kat West. The cast was as follows:

AUROCH.....................................Carolyn Baeumler

MEG ....Jordan Baker

JAMES ....Peter Bradbury

BEN ....Jon Krupp

VERONICA ....Anna Kull

MATT...Noah Robbins

CHARACTERS

MEG – mid-40s/50s, savvy, educated, from the country

BEN – mid-40/50s, idealistic, from the city (the Bronx, but no accent)

MATT – 14, emerging; born on the farm, but smart

JAMES – mid-40s/50s, a businessman from the city, polished, aggressive but ultimately fragile

VERONICA – 15, searching; has had to grow up a little too fast; from the city

AUROCH – like Meg, but wilder – and quite possibly the last living wild cow

SETTING

A dairy farm upon a hill, western Massachusetts.

The set should contain an old farm kitchen, classic, untouched by time except for the occasional 1980s replacement appliance. Nothing digital! A large table is at the center of the room.

A back-door leads from the kitchen to a small back porch with steps leading into the yard.

In the yard, is the façade of an old barn, which can be shifted to the interior wall of the barn, with proper lighting.

A wooden fence with a gate separates the yard from the fields and the wilderness.

The play is set within a vast expanse of rolling hills. When the actors view these, they look somewhere out at the back of the audience. However, the set might contain some suggestion of these hills in the background.

TIME

Summer, 1984

AUTHOR'S NOTES

Lighting plays a special role in this play. The "interior" moments are encapsulated glimpses into the interior of each character—his or her "inner sound track", if you will. These moments express the essence that these characters keep within themselves and struggle to express—the things that language cannot capture. These moments are the key to the link between the naturalistic tone and the more stylized realms of the play.

The lighting for the fence scenes (Auroch/Meg) is similar, yet slightly different, to the "interior" lighting; by the end, these two lighting motifs merge for the final tableau.

In the play, there are moments when Auroch remains onstage, observing a scene, trying to understand how domesticated beings survive. She can react to what's going on, but she should not steal focus from the scene.

I like the idea that as the play progresses, the physical world of the set comes apart as the walls between domestic and wild come down. By the end, I envision all that exists of the kitchen is the table, standing alone in the wilderness. Director Jessica Bauman and set designer Susan Zeeman Rogers found a brilliant variation on this idea for the New York City production. The idea can be played upon, or not, in future productions.

There are times in the script when the end of a character's line has a word in [brackets]. This is the word the character would speak if he or she weren't interrupted by the next speaker.

In playing the final few scenes, we discovered it is best not to think of them as multiple endings, but rather as a series of unfolding new beginnings. We found this was the key to keeping the ending sequence active.

SPECIAL THANKS

To Joann S. Grohman for the invaluable insights and inspiration I gleaned from her book *Keeping a Family Cow* and for her generosity in allowing me to quote from it. To Hawthorne Valley Farm, Rachel Schneider and all the cows, for bringing us into their fold. To Jessica Bauman for her ongoing belief in, dedication to, and development of the play. To New Georges, especially Susan Bernfield for her amazing support as a friend and producer. To the Orchard Project, the Lark Play Development Center and the Good Writers Group for their vital roles in developing the play. To the NYC cast and other dedicated actors who lent themselves to, and have become part of, these characters: Melissa Leo, Heidi Armbruster, Matthew Stadelmann, Kelly AuCoin, Katie Barrett, Mark Zeisler, Brandon Kruhm, Christopher Randolph, Christopher Burns, Dale Soules and Allyn Burrows. To the girls on Barnum Street, for always saying hello. And very special thanks to Joe Roland, for roaming beside me.

MILK is dedicated to William and Dorothy DeVoti,
my parents and friends,
who taught me all the values worth hanging on to.

ACT 1

(INTERIOR: AUROCH)

(Heavy wind, carrying the distant mooing of cows.)

(From the darkness, AUROCH, a woman, appears on the far side of the fence. The wind blows her untamed hair. The image is not unlike an 80s album cover. She gazes towards the farmhouse. A window-paned square of light gradually illuminates her face.)

(She cocks her head to listen to the cows, sniffs at the wind.)

(From inside, we hear 80s music on a transistor radio, scratchy reception. Static, as someone changes stations. An NPR show tunes in and out.*)

(Lights/sound begins to fade on AUROCH, up on:)

---

*Please see Music Use Note on Page 3.

Scene One

(BEN and MEG sit at a long kitchen table, lit by the bright white light of a kerosene lantern. Ledgers and papers are spread out before them. MEG works on the ledgers. BEN fiddles with a small battery-op radio with a metal clothes hanger for an antenna. The radio underscores the scene.)

VOICE OF REAGAN. *(soundbite) (scratchy radio sounds, then)* "Trees cause more pollution than automobiles do."

VOICE OF COMMENTATOR. That's from the last – from the 1980 campaign, the primaries in New Hampshire. What do you want to say about that quote, David?

VOICE OF TALKING HEAD. Well, he was elected, wasn't he?!

(cronyism chuckling, gives way to static)

Listen – the first thing I want to say, is: I'm tired of defending the President, Bob. "Pollution from trees kills more people than automobiles." "There are fifty taxes on a loaf of bread." I mean, of course these things aren't true. But you know what? I think that the American people don't care. They LIKE Reagan. They TRUST Reagan –

(scratchy radio sound)

MEG. I don't think we're gonna get any real news on this station, Ben. Better try AM.

BEN. I'm trying. The switch is stuck.

VOICE OF TALKING HEAD. I think the answer is: don't try to see every one of these stories as, well, "absolute truth." "Trees cause pollution." "COWS cause pollution – "

MEG. *What* did he say?

VOICE OF TALKING HEAD. "Backing the contras in Nicaragua is good neighbor policy." ... *(static)* ..."AIDS is a myth." ... *(static)*

MEG. Did he say COWS cause –

VOICE OF TALKING HEAD. "Top-heavy wealth will trickle down"...

MEG. Really, Ben, the barn roof is about to blow off, and –

VOICE OF TALKING HEAD. "Ice cream and jelly beans are health food" –

MEG. all you can listen to is –

BEN. I'm trying, Meg. I'm –

MEG. Don't force it. Here, let me –

BEN. FUCK. It snapped – Damn it!

VOICE OF TALKING HEAD. They may sound like "lies," Bob, but that's close-minded. Here in Washington, we prefer to call them "parables." You see, you've got to remember the importance of parables in life. Our country does – They understand the things Reagan says are stories pointing to larger truths, rather than stories that are necessarily, you know, grounded in day-to-day reality. I mean, Hell, he remembers things out of movies that he thinks actually happened, and… people just don't seem to mind…

(scratchy buzz of radio changing stations)

BEN. I got the *dial* moving… that's a start…

(A Top 40 song.* SNAP. Scratchy station changing.)

It needed a Phillips, not the flat head to get that baby –

*(Commercial: a plumbing store, tanning salon…**BEN** is about to change stations –)*

MEG. No, no – this is it. Wait. I think this is –

VOICE OF WEATHERMAN. …again… *(static)* High wind advisory – *(static)* Litchfield – Columb[ia] – *(static)* … drought conditions contin[ue] – *(static)* …strong winds at 75 m.p.h.…humidity zero.

BEN. Useless.

VOICE OF WEATHERMAN. *(oddly clear)* Hold onto your cows!

MEG. "Hold onto your –" Did he just say that?

(beat)

I swear, I think I hear things sometimes, Ben. *Erroneous* things.

---

*Please see Music Use Note on page 3.

(Light shift: kerosene light extends to further reaches of the farmhouse kitchen.)

BEN. When the damn weatherman starts to get a sense of humor, you know we're all in trouble.

MEG. Everyone's a standup comic these days – from the guy at the dump to the girl at the checkout –

BEN. *(referring to the radio)* I think I'm gonna have to take this thing apart.

MEG. Everyone's got something to say.

(back to the radio)

Wait till the electric comes back on at least, ok?

BEN. No, I think I'll take apart our only news source by torchlight. Jesus, Meg, sometimes you –

(trying to avoid a fight)

Well. Nothing wrong with comedy. As long as they can crack jokes and work at the same time.

MEG. Well, no – They can't: work, joke. I always have to check my receipt against that girl "Becky" at the A&P. Half the time? I've got to go back. I always figure my list against what's in checking, you know – I can get this, but not that, put that back to get this... There was one time, she charged me 11.99/lb for bologna. Twelve dollars, for bologna? If I pay that, I'm gonna get caviar or at least a donation to Green Peace.

BEN. We can't afford –

MEG. I was joking, Ben. I know we can't.

BEN. You should report her.

MEG. I can check my bill afterwards. It won't kill me. Besides, sometimes she makes mistakes in my favor. And when she spots me in line? If she's got a new joke? I can see her start to prep. Her whole body gets straight and poised and READY, to really give it her all. It's kind of beautiful.

BEN. You're just trying to distract her, so you can get a deal.

MEG. Cynic.

BEN. Am I wrong?

MEG. She's got something, Ben. A – I don't know – a spark, a *dream* –

BEN. Is she a Robin Williams? Joan Rivers? Give her a real break, Meg. Tell her the truth. At least when she becomes a single mother on welfare, she'll be able to balance someone's books.

(**MEG** *is struck viscerally; she's been balancing their books all evening.*)

MEG. Don't need to be single, to balance books.

(*Beat.* **BEN** *softens.*)

BEN. Help me out here, Meg.

MEG. I just do the counting.

BEN. Check it again.

MEG. I've checked it eight times.

BEN. Please.

(*She checks it. He looks over her shoulder. She flinches, then softens, smiles, lets him stay. She finishes her numbers, lays down the calculator. He looks away.*)

MEG. There's something so satisfying about numbers. If you do it right, they always turn out exactly the same.

BEN. How can you be so calm?

MEG. It's not us.

BEN. Two hundred years your family holds onto this place –

MEG. It's just a ledger. Accounts –

BEN. And then I come along, and blow the whole –

MEG. *You* didn't blow anything, Ben. My dad was the best milk farmer you have *ever* –

BEN. Thanks.

MEG. He *started earlier,* is all I'm saying. Earlier in life.

BEN. (*said like someone who's long lived in someone else's shadow*) He was the best.

MEG. All I mean is – even *he* wouldn't know how to hold on. Not now. Not in these – Paper says 35 farms a day are – 35! Lights out. What do we have that they don't have? Breathtaking views, sky-rocketing taxes, Midwest dairies consolidating, slushing in "product" – have you noticed? it's not "milk" anymore, it's "product" – interest rates through the roof – we owe more now than when we first took out the damn loans –

(She chokes up, contains it. Strongly, she points out the window:)

And hundreds of arable acres, primed and ready for the developer to –

BEN. Don't talk that way.

MEG. Someone has to. Things change, Ben. They don't want us anymore. Our farm, our form, it's…disappearing.

BEN. It's who we are.

MEG. I don't think that's true.

BEN. You, the land, the kids – it's all one, in my mind, I can't distinguish them, I –

MEG. *(angrily)* Well, you're gonna have to, won't you?

(beat)

This isn't us, either…this not-getting-along?

(She looks outside at the swirling dust.)

It's raining out there somewhere. It just dries up before it hits the ground.

*(**MATT** enters. He wears his Walkman, like a permanent appendage.)*

MATT. Hey. What are you guys doing sitting in the dark?

BEN. The electricity is out, if you haven't noticed.

MEG. Hi, honey.

*(**MATT** bends down and kisses her.)*

MATT. It's been on for the past thirty-seven minutes, if you haven't noticed. No, I guess you haven't, 'cause everything in this kitchen is FIFTY YEARS OLD. The clocks come back on, who's gonna notice? I have three syllables for you: "di-gi-tal." Here, and the mail.

(He drops it on the table.)

And he said: "Let there be light!"

(He flips on the switch as he exits. It's a little bit blinding. They squint.)

MEG. At least he knows his syllables.

BEN. And his scripture. Smart-ass kid.

*(**BEN** extinguishes the lantern, moves to hang it on its nail across the room.)*

MEG. Yeah, well, teenagers…

BEN. Maybe if he worked the land a little harder –

MEG. – he'd grow up to be a farmer just like you?

BEN. Point made.

MEG. Now's not the time, Ben.

BEN. I said, point made.

(pause)

He'd learn some values, is all I meant.

MEG. Couldn't leave it, could you?

BEN. Lessons from the [land] –

MEG. What – to be the dirty-nailed, cowshit-smelling bumpkin in the classroom? For the last time, Ben, farming isn't some experiment in ethics. It's your profession –

BEN. "For the last time." That's quite a thing to say.

*(Beat. They feel bad about the bickering. **BEN** sorts the mail.)*

MEG. Anything good?

BEN. Bills, catalogues…

*(**MEG** picks up a catalogue.)*

Don't even think –

MEG. It's free to look.

*(**BEN** opens an envelope, reads. **MEG** checks and circles items.)*

*(**BEN** suddenly gets very pale.)*

BEN. Meg?

MEG. What.

(**BEN** *doesn't answer.* **MEG** *looks up, sees something is off.*)

Ben, what is it?

BEN. A letter.

MEG. Did someone die?

BEN. No, it's…Business.

MEG. Great. Now they're sending personal notes. Who thought I'd ever be nostalgic for form letters. Who's it from?

BEN. *(distracted, reading)* Some guy…

MEG. Yeah, well of course it's from a *guy.* They're always – I mean, which *company*?

BEN. No, it's not from a company, it's – listen, it doesn't matter *who* he is. He…how can I say this. He…wants to buy us.

MEG. Oh. *That.* Two minutes ago, selling wasn't exactly something to –

BEN. Not *the farm*, we can *keep* that, but…The *right*, to bring his family here, that's all, to…"collaborate" in our "living atmosphere," that's what he says – "living atmosphere," who talks like that? – to show them…"how real people live."

MEG. Oh, that's ridiculous.

(She grabs the first page of the letter.)

BEN. He wants to teach his kids, to let the *land* – Here, see?

MEG. *(reading)* "I have every confidence they can learn to hang out at the mall and shop when they're 18. Meanwhile, I want them to be somewhere that tests their developmental skills. To teach them some values."

BEN. Smart man.

(**MEG** *gives him a sharp look.*)

His lawyer will work out the details, a "formality" really…

MEG. I'm not a circus.

BEN. It's a lot of money.

MEG. For someone to drop in and just –

> *(He hands her the second page. Her jaw drops.)*

> It's not right. It's too much. There's something…

> *(pause)*

> Why us?

BEN. Spent a summer in the area when he was a kid. Used to walk up here all the time, loved the view, keeps thinking of it… "Pure"… "Untouched"… blah blah blah…the point is, he's got money.

MEG. There's something not right about it.

BEN. He sounds perfectly reasonable.

MEG. That's just it. It's uncanny –

BEN. What could not be –

MEG. He SOUNDS LIKE YOU.

BEN. What? You think I – ?

MEG. No, I just. How did he know what you want?

BEN. A weekend here, a week there –

MEG. What you've always – ?

BEN. We can really pay it off. The loans, the mortgage –

MEG. I don't like it.

BEN. We can really *own* it again.

> *(beat)*

> Besides, a meeting, he just wants – We're not committing, not yet, it's just a – Jesus, it's a gift from God, is what it is.

MEG. It sounds like a deal with the Devil, if you want my opinion.

> *(pause)*

> Wait a minute.

BEN. What?

MEG. It's Sunday, Ben. We don't get mail on Sundays.

> *(Lights shift:)*

Scene Two

(Sound of a helicopter. At the fence: **JAMES**, *in business casual, neatly pressed. His stiff hair starts to lift and blow, as he steps away from the wind force of the chopper blades. The chopper disembarks on the far side of the fence.)*

*(***JAMES*** looks around, taking it in. He removes a book from his breast pocket, reads:)*

JAMES. "Dairying in its most reductionist form, *merely swiping some milk from a cooperative grazing animal…*goes so many thousands of years back into pre-history…that we can't get a fix on it."

(He walks through the fence, which gives way easily to his touch, and starts walking across the stage, looking around.)

(Light shift: **BEN** *joins* **JAMES**, *giving him the tour.* **MEG** *trails behind.* **AUROCH** *kind of grazes, watching curiously from the field.)*

BEN. This is my favorite spot. I come here at least once a day, once a day for eighteen years, and – it always surprises me, how beautiful it is. The slope of the hill right there, I love that. You should see it in autumn… the way it leads into all the other hills, layer on layer of them. On a clear day you can… Can you? Nooo, not… quite, not today…but, on a really clear day – you can see straight through to Vermont –

JAMES. It's just like I remembered…as a boy, only…to finally get *inside*, it's…

*(***JAMES*** takes a deep breath, to take it all in.)*

I hope you don't take this the wrong way, but – that… smell, is it always quite so – ?

(They look at him, puzzled.)

You…don't…smell anything.

*(***BEN*** *and* **MEG** *look at each other, perplexed.)*

(uncomfortable pause)

MEG. Ohhhh,…Cows. He means –

BEN. OH. *That.* Well, it's a dairy farm.

JAMES. Isn't there any way to –

BEN. They live here.

JAMES. Oh… Right.

BEN. You get used to it.

(pause)

JAMES. Really is some view.

BEN. Sure is. Black and white cows speckled across the green… Well, it's sort of green. It's green when we've got water. But the cows – black and white. *They* don't change.

JAMES. Everyone seems to have them around here…the black and white ones.

BEN. Classic. Holsteins.

MEG. Best milkers, hands down.

JAMES. I'm sure they are. But you know, I was thinking…

BEN. Great! We always like to hear your thoughts. That's what it's about. "Collaboration!"

*(**MEG** rolls her eyes.)*

JAMES. Great. Because I have some ideas. Have you ever seen those cows, bulls maybe: shaggy, brown, I don't know what they're called… They look like…buffalo?

BEN. Oh, you mean…Scottish Highlands?

*(**BEN** starts laughing at the thought of them; he can't help it.)*

JAMES. I've been looking. No one has them.

BEN. That's because they're not really good for anything. And they look so ridic –

JAMES. I like them. They're like…the Wild West. Like – tumbleweed.

BEN. Well, you've come the right year for *that*…

JAMES. Like…SHAG carpet.

MEG. They're not milking cows. They're meat cows.

JAMES. I think we need some.

MEG. We're a milking farm.

JAMES. *(laughs, charmed)* Oh, you don't have to do that anymore.

MEG. What are you talking about?

JAMES. I mean, you can, of course, if you like it, if it makes you feel better. We can have both, but –

MEG. *(firmly)* We are a milking farm.

JAMES. And that pays for itself?

    (beat)

    So, then, what's the difference? I'll buy them. Don't worry about that. I'm thinking a dozen bulls – the males are more impressive, wild, hairy, horned, masculine, really fierce.

MEG. In with our GIRLS?

JAMES. Oh, they'll get along fine.

MEG. Male bulls, female cows? Right next to each other…?

JAMES. That's why God created fences.

BEN. Let me play Devil's advocate for a minute –

MEG. Isn't that what you've *been* doing?

BEN. *(ignoring her)* Have you ever tried to keep bulls, from cows in heat, with a *fence?*

JAMES. You have steel, don't you?

BEN. Well, yeah, but –

JAMES. Don't tell me there's nothing man can do, in all his infinite wisdom, to keep cows and bulls from breeding. No material strong enough? No wall high enough? Really, Ben, I thought you were a modern man. You sound like a downright romantic. How do you keep your bulls separate now?

BEN. Artificial insemination has always been just fine for our girls.

JAMES. You don't even HAVE bulls?

BEN. I'm a real pro.

JAMES. Well, then this is going to be a real treat for those girls.

MEG. Oh, Jesus.

BEN. 87 percent success rate on the first go. You can check those numbers –

MEG. You have no idea what it's like to handle a –

BEN. *(overlapping)* – beats the hell out of a –

MEG & BEN. – live bull.

JAMES. Okay, so let's back up. Say they mate? So what? Think outside the box. I wonder what we'd get.

MEG. Oh, I don't know…"Mutts"?

JAMES. A "hybrid." Half domestic, half wild. I bet we could market them.

MEG. And call them what, The Suburban?

(Beat. BEN *tries to serve as calm rational peacemaker.)*

BEN. What Meg means is – Let me explain. Holsteins, the "black and white ones" –

JAMES. Are common.

MEG. Yes. And do you know why?

JAMES. Because people around here lack innovation.

MEG. No. Because they work. The cows. They –

(with determined patience) See, Holsteins – "Holstein-Friesians" – have been bred down to the finest pedigree, for their maximum milking potential, for their smart yet docile personalities, for their particular constitutional match with the New England climate and soil. They're like a perfect, natural machine. Nature does that sometimes, creates perfection – with a little guidance, of course. It's…kind of amazing, don't you think?

JAMES. *(not listening)* Sedate, domestic, circa 1950, when I look out, that's what I see. I want something wild. Buffalo. Indians. The frontier. We need to shake things up around here.

MEG. Things are fine as they are.

JAMES. What, are you afraid of change?

MEG. No, I –

(Beat. He's nailed her.)

JAMES. I've been reading this book.

(He taps the book in his pocket.)

Did you know – the cow is the only domestic animal that has no wild population pool? Here: "The last known wild cow, called an 'auroch,' died over 500 years ago in Poland." "Like corn, the staple of the Aztecs that now exists only as farm seed, she has no wild sisters."

MEG. *(surprisingly moved)* "She has no wild…"?

JAMES. Your docile "Holstein-Friesian"… I bet she can't even remember what that feels like, to be wild…

*(This really gets under **MEG**'s skin; she doesn't know why.)*

*(**AUROCH** peers towards the book with cow-like curiosity.)*

MEG. What book is that?

(She grabs for it.)

JAMES. Just a book.

(He slips it back into his pocket.)

MEG. Why don't you just go find a farm out West?

*(**BEN** shoots her a desperate look.)*

JAMES. Because I want this one.

(beat)

But that was just an idea. We're just – "brainstorming" here, that's all. No harm in it. I have lots of ideas, it's my way. It's your farm. My way, your farm, we'll… That's how business works, we throw things out there. The details are in the contract.

BEN. *(a little over-eager)* So, do we have a deal?

JAMES. Has there ever been a question?

(He smiles winningly and holds out his hand.)

(MEG looks disgusted.)

(BEN takes it, shakes.)

(JAMES holds his hand out to MEG. She indicates her hand is dirty.)

MEG. Sorry, I was just shoveling.

(JAMES smiles, surfacely. MEG turns away. BEN is uncomfortable.)

JAMES. Well, I guess that's that.

(He's done here. He starts to look at his watch, the sky, his watch…)

MEG. Aren't…you forgetting something?

(He looks at her blankly.)

Your daughter? She's still back in the barn.

JAMES. Oh, right. I forgot.

BEN. She must sure like cows!

MEG. She found a place to sit and listen to her Walkman.

BEN. I guess she and Matt will have something in common then.

MEG. Maybe you should…I don't know…get her?

(As JAMES exits, AUROCH steals the book from his pocket. She leans on the gate and starts to browse through it.)

MEG. He "forgot?" The one he's so hot to educate?

BEN. Maybe he was distracted by your rudeness. Really – you could have shaken his hand, Meg.

MEG. They were dirty.

BEN. They're not –

MEG. Full of shit?

(beat)

Shaggy cows? Cowboys and Indians? Come on, Ben.

BEN. It's business, Meg. You have to bend a little. On the little things. Bend or break. Don't break on the little things. You'd never make it out there.

MEG. What, in the wild, rangy, primitive world of business? I'm in the business of cows, not sheep – there used to be a difference.

(**JAMES** *returns with his daughter,* **VERONICA.**)

JAMES. Veronica's going to stay with you till I come back, if that's okay.

MEG. Oh! I didn't expect –

(**VERONICA** *looks embarrassed.* **MEG** *softens.*)

Of course. I'll have Matt show her the way to – You can have Jenny's room. That's our daugher, she – Well, it's hers when she comes to visit, she's in college, but it's yours while – You'd like her, Jenny. I mean, I don't know you, but – well, I like her. MATT. MATT!

(*The sound of the chopper again.*)

(**JAMES** *looks at his watch, grits his teeth.*)

JAMES. 97 seconds late.

BEN. So, we'll see you next week?

JAMES. Friday, 6 sharp. I should have a new pilot by then.

MEG. And you'll bring the rest of your family, right?

(**VERONICA** *shoots him a look.*)

You do…have a family, right? Or…didya forget?

(*uncomfortable pause*)

Joke.

(*No one says anything.*)

Okay. Dinner's at 7. Three of us, five of you. You've got two brothers and a mom, right, Veronica?

(*She looks at* **JAMES** *as she asks the question. Then back at* **VERONICA***:*)

What…do you all like to eat?

JAMES. Don't go out of your way for us. As you can see, we're easy. Whatever you eat.

(*Pause. He surveys his property one last time.*)

You people look so much nicer than I thought you would.

MEG. Oh. Thanks –

JAMES. No, I mean… You shouldn't dress up for us –

MEG. Oh, no, this is what we normally –

JAMES. No, I mean… don't you…dress a little rougher, to work?

(pause)

Like I said, don't go to any special bother for me, but –

MEG. Something a little more rustic.

JAMES. If it's not too much out of your way.

*(The helicopter begins its descent; their hair blows from the vortex centerstage. **MATT** comes into the field, carrying a pan of milk. He looks up at the chopper.)*

MATT. Cool.

MEG. Matt, bring Veronica to your sister's room.

MATT. All right.

VERONICA. Wait, my bags.

MATT. Your what?

VERONICA. You know…baggage.

(Two enormous bags drop down – presumably from the chopper – with a thud.)

MATT. Oh.

*(**MATT** just stands looking at them. He doesn't know what to do. **VERONICA** looks at him expectantly. He smiles uneasily, goes to lift one. It's really heavy.)*

BEN. See, if you'd lifted some more of those grain sacks, you'd be ready for this.

*(good-naturedly, to **JAMES**)*

Don't worry. We'll do better with *your* kids –

*(**MATT** tries one of the bags again, and just manages to lift it. He decides to just drag it. He puts his headphones on and starts walking towards the house. **VERONICA** puts her headphones on and follows him. They exit.)*

*(**MATT** leaves his pan of milk.)*

BEN. Hey, wait – try some fresh milk before you go. We use machines, mostly, but Matt's working up his milking muscles, you know, in his hands. His cow's gonna calf soon, and he'll hand milk her. BC – that's his cow. Raised her since she was a little thing. Kind of a 4H project. Name's Buttercup, but that embarrasses him, so we call her –

(**MEG** *shoots him a look.*)

What? Meg give him some, will you? We're a little worried, BC, she's got a weak heart, but – Hey, what's the good of a dairy cow if she can't deliver?

(**MEG** *lifts the pan, and, unwillingly, hands it to* **JAMES.**)

You ever tasted fresh milk? Non-pasteurized, non-homogenized.

JAMES. That doesn't sound particularly hygienic.

BEN. Just like nature meant you to drink it.

(**MEG** *hands him the pan.*)

MEG. Don't let the pail touch your lips.

JAMES. I thought your hands were –

MEG. *(smiling "nicely")* That's why.

(*He holds up the pan and drops some milk into his mouth.*)

(*And immediately spits it out.*)

JAMES. Uch, it's warm.

(**MEG** *can't help smiling, entertained, but also a bit superior. Her teaching/mothering instincts kick in.*)

MEG. It always tastes strange the first time. You have to open your mind to it. Try it again.

(*He does. This time he closes his eyes, and really drinks. Its starts to flow over his face a little. He is in ecstasy. Lights begin to shift slightly, to "interior" lighting. Alarmed, **MEG** pulls the milk out of his hands. Lights return to normal.*)

(JAMES *looks at* MEG, *milk in the corners of his mouth, with the imprinted look of a baby duck on its mother.*)

JAMES. Wow.

(MEG *looks uncomfortable.*)

BEN. Well, see you next week, Mr. –

JAMES. Oh, please – Mister's my father's name. Call me James. We're friends here.

BEN. Great.

JAMES. Bye, Meg.

(MEG *turns away.*)

BEN. Next week, Jim!

JAMES. James.

BEN. Right. See you!

(JAMES *looks at* MEG, *pulls himself together and walks into the chopper wind, his stiff hair again lifting in the force of the wind.*)

(BEN *follows him with his eyes and watches as the chopper ascends.*)

BEN. Now, that wasn't so bad, was it? He just needs to settle in. I think he'll be just fine. Did you see the way he took to that milk? No one ever takes to it so fast as that.

MEG. I feel strange, Ben.

BEN. What?

MEG. I don't know. Like, not myself. Like, things are changing, like –

(AUROCH *moos, low and haunting, from beyond the fence. The moo reverberates, blended with something faintly mythical.* MEG *hears it;* BEN *appears not to.*)

BEN. I thought that's what you wanted.

MEG. I don't know, I –

(*Another moo.* MEG *doesn't know where it came from. She looks towards the field, then peers down as if within herself. Lights begin a slow but sure shift to "interior" lighting:*)

Did you hear that?

BEN. What?

(Beat. Transition. Complete shift to interior lighting:)

(interior: family)

(Middle of the night. A cow moos in the barn, giving birth – long, low, labored.)

*(A "fire-line" of buckets. **MEG** fills one bucket at a time from a combination of pots on the stove [for birthing]. **MATT** takes each bucket, carries it to the door, where **BEN** takes the bucket, disappears. Then reappears for the next one. Etc.)*

(They don't speak. It's the well-oiled mechanism of a family, working.)

*(The moos begin to diminish, in a weakening sort of way. The urgency of the fire-line increases. There is a final strong moo. **BEN** stops in the door, turns to look back at **MATT**, who stops in his tracks.)*

(Lights shift to:)

Scene Three

(MATT sits on the couch, rigid, listening to his Walkman. MEG sits next to him.)

MEG. Sweetheart...

(He doesn't answer. Gently, she taps him. He flinches.)

(She gestures to his headset. He hits "stop.")

It's okay. To feel this way?

MATT. I'm fine.

MEG. It's life. One big, wide –

(She draws a circle in the air.)

You can cry, you know.

MATT. I said I'm fine.

MEG. It's funny, how it happens. I mean, not FUNNY, but – in families. When you were born, your great aunt Hettie died. Just two days later. And with Jenny, it was Dad, my dad. It's almost like – Souls have to go somewhere! And when a new body comes into it...well, it's part of our job, to give up our old ones... Besides, those new bodies look so tempting. I think some of those old souls *jump* at the chance...to begin again, you know? A clean slate. You were good to BC, honey.

MATT. It's just a cow, Mom, don't be so dramatic.

MEG. She would want you to be good to that calf.

MATT. I already raised a calf, I –

MEG. She would want you to love that calf like it was her.

MATT. I don't want a calf, Mom. Okay? I'm sick of raising calves.

MEG. Okay.

MATT. I'm sick of hanging out in the barn.

MEG. Well, there are other things we can do –

MATT. No, not "we," ME. I want to do things alone, okay?

MEG. Okay. Well –

MATT. And I want a television. In my room. In *color*. Do you
know, all those times we watched *The Wizard of Oz*, I
never knew it turned to color? Everyone else did! Do
you know how embarrassing that was? And I want an
IZOD shirt, a real one, not the fake kind. And Stan
Smiths – Do you even know what Stan Smiths ARE?
They're sneakers, the *right* sneakers – YOU CAN'T
GET THEM AT K-Mart, okay? And...

MEG. Okay.

MATT. And...

MEG. Ok. I'll – I'll...

MATT. And...

MEG. I'll try.

*(He turns to her finally, and sobs into her chest. She
holds him. Tears trickle down her face.)*

We all have a weak spot, honey. We try to protect it,
with people we love. Maybe we should have with BC.
I don't know. I don't know. I don't.... Let it never get
tested.

*(JAMES emerges from the shadows and watches them,
galvanized.)*

*(MEG looks up and sees him, jolts, but holds MATT closer
so he doesn't see.)*

(mouths) Do you...mind?

(JAMES doesn't look away.)

*(MEG reaches down and presses "play" on MATT's
Walkman.)*

This...is private.

(JAMES stays there, watching.)

(MEG leads MATT into the next room.)

(She returns, alone.)

What do you want?

(He doesn't say anything.)

MEG. *(cont.)* I know what you're thinking. Sitting here, sobbing over a cow...? Look at you – Have you ever had an emotion in your life? A real, pure – I'm proud of that boy. To raise a boy who can – feel like that, who can –

(Her voice breaks.)

We're all a little tired. It was grueling – We're all a little...

(He comes and sits beside her. They sit together, in silence. A comfortable moment. He leans closer. The moment turns uncomfortable.)

How...was your week?

*(**JAMES** puts his head on **MEG**'s breast.)*

(Lights momentarily shift to:)

*(Interior: **JAMES**)*

(a moment)

(awkward pause)

(Lights flicker back to normal:)

*(**MEG** gets up, abruptly dumps **JAMES**.)*

(They stare each other down.)

(She exits. Lights.)

Scene Four

(Interior: **VERONICA***)*

(She stands in the field, alone, with field weeds.)

(The fence: **AUROCH** *leans against it, chewing rhythmically, reading* **JAMES***'s book with personal interest.)*

AUROCH. *(reading)* "Two factors are absent in the life of a calf separated from its mother. One, is happiness. A calf needs lots of interaction to thrive. If there is somebody in the family with time to provide this, well and good. But the mother cow showers her calf with enthusiastic attention and teaches it a lot of cow things. The calf develops a huge will to live."

(She peers across the fence, curiously.)

(Lights fade down on **AUROCH**, *up on:)*

*(***MATT** *sits on the fence, listening to his Walkman. He wears very dark sunglasses.)*

*(***VERONICA** *enters, wearing an old over-big T-shirt, carrying her field weeds.)*

VERONICA. Hey.

*(***MATT** *hits "stop" on his Walkman.)*

MATT. Hey.

VERONICA. What…'s your future so bright?

MATT. Huh?

VERONICA. The shades.

MATT. Oh. Uh…no. Bee sting.

(She sits next to him. Pause.)

What are you doing?

VERONICA. Sitting next to you.

MATT. No, I mean –

VERONICA. I was out in the field. I've never been in one.

MATT. You haven't?

VERONICA. It's amazing.

MATT. It *is?*

VERONICA. Yeah. I mean, there's all kinds of things out there. Bugs, birds, little...holes, in the dirt. Flowers –

MATT. Those are weeds.

VERONICA. There was this thing? A squirrel? That's what I thought, at first, but – it had this fur, it's so much softer and...*richer*, you know? The color. And its face, that's different. Like – a *weasel*, that's what I thought when I looked at it: *weasel*. I mean, I've never – well, maybe at the Museum of Natural History, on a field trip, but – It's like it was sleeping. I mean, it was dead, is dead, but – It was so cool, to be able to look at it so close like that. It was so flat. I've never – Its fur was so beautiful.

MATT. Could have been a mink.

VERONICA. They run wild?

MATT. Sure. Sometimes.

VERONICA. Wow.

(pause)

I want to visit it every day.

MATT. It's dead.

VERONICA. Yeah.

MATT. You're twisted.

VERONICA. You should come with me. You can't even tell, almost, that it's –

MATT. Dead.

VERONICA. Yeah.

MATT. No thanks.

VERONICA. When you look close, you can see these teeny little perforations around its neck. Like a necklace. That's where the flies are. Not many, but – that's what made me look and see the marks. Otherwise, it – looks totally peaceful.

(beat)

I can't talk to you, like that, like – when I can't see your eyes.

MATT. Okay.

(Pause. He presses "play" on his Walkman again.)

(She reaches for the button, fakes him out and knocks his glasses off.)

(His eyes are super puffy. He covers his face, freezes; he doesn't know what to do.)

VERONICA. That was some bee.

MATT. Yeah, it was.

VERONICA. Both eyes?

MATT. I'm...allergic.

VERONICA. That only happens to me when I've been crying.

MATT. Yeah, well...you must not be allergic.

(He finally gets his glasses back from her and puts them on.)

VERONICA. Do you always listen to that?

MATT. Yeah.

VERONICA. Me too.

MATT. It's not enough, though.

VERONICA. *(surprised)* I know what you mean.

MATT. I wanna see it, too. Have you ever seen it? You know, MTV?

VERONICA. Oh, *that*... Yeah. Sure.

MATT. You *have*? What's it like?

VERONICA. You know, music, videos. It's...I don't know, you listen to the song and then you see stuff. Which one?

MATT. "I Wanna New Drug," Huey Lewis.

VERONICA. Uck.

MATT. What?

VERONICA. Why do you want to know?

MATT. I – guess I want to know what I'm supposed to see when I hear it. I mean, I listen to it, all the time, but –

VERONICA. Well, what do *you* see?

MATT. Uh...

VERONICA. Everyone's supposed to see something different, inside, when they hear it, that's the point – that's what music's about.

MATT. Then why did they make a music video, duh?

VERONICA. Because – Oh, okay, fine. But I don't think I can remember that one.

MATT. I'll sing it for you.

(Matt sings the first verse of a rock song, something like "I Want A New Drug" by Huey Lewis. He sings poorly, but passionately.)

VERONICA. *(laughing)* Ok, you know what. That's actually kind of not inspiring? I remember. So – the music, you hear that, *in your head,* and then – you see him singing.

MATT. What's he look like?

VERONICA. Pale, skinny, dark hair, white T-shirt, black leather jacket…He's on the tape jacket, you know what he looks like.

MATT. I just thought – Okay, whatever. Then what?

VERONICA. He's in his apartment, somewhere kind of skuzzy, you know, "downtown" "cool"…some closet, bare white walls, roaches, rust in the water. Got it? And it's his face, and he's singing, and then he's, you know, kind of thrashing through his bare refrigerator looking for *drugs* – but all he finds are *ice cubes* – so he throws them in a sink full of water, and sticks his face in it, and then it's like this *underwater point of view* – his face, it's in the water, it's in the *camera,* but – it's like he's singing at *you, to you:*

*(VERONICA starts to sing the last verse of the rock song. MATT joins her. They get pulled into the song and really give it their all.)**
(beat)

VERONICA. *(defensively)* It's not like I've ever actually *watched it,* you know – it just…*comes on.* There's not many of them. The same one runs like every hour.

---

* Please see Music Use Note on Page 3.

MATT. You ever...done them?

VERONICA. What?

MATT. You know...drugs.

VERONICA. Well, *yeah*. Sure.

MATT. You have?

VERONICA. It's, you know, something to do.

MATT. Oh. Right.

VERONICA. ...Haven't you?

MATT. Sure. I just thought – you know, that they...only had them in the country.

VERONICA. Only had drugs in the country?

MATT. Uh, yeah. What's your favorite?

VERONICA. Well, pot's good for kind of every day, you know.

MATT. Definitely.

VERONICA. But coke – that's wild. We do that sometimes on weekends, or like Thursdays? – it totally gets you through school on Friday. You can stay up all night, and before you know it, it's sunrise and wham! There it is! Sun! And I'm still up, and I'm still up, and I'm... and then I sleep for like two days straight. You totally and completely crash, like – like nothing could keep you awake, just like for those two nights nothing could get you down, suddenly, you – you've just got to give in and disappear, into it, sleep. It's like – you're dead. I guess. It's – great. Well, it's different. It wasn't so great, but it's – something. You know?

MATT. Yeah, I – I feel that way about it, too.

VERONICA. But I don't do them anymore, drugs. They're bad, they – You don't do them anymore, do you?

(Pause. He doesn't really know what to say.)

Don't.

MATT. Okay.

VERONICA. I'm over that phase of my life.

MATT. Uh, yeah. Me, too.

(beat)

Where'd you get that shirt?

VERONICA. I got milk on mine, out in the barn. Your dad brought me to look at the – well, the calf. And I held the bottle, and – So your mom gave me this.

MATT. It's my *mom's?*

VERONICA. Yeah. Why?

MATT. Don't you have one of your own? I mean, you brought two HUGE suitcases, don't you have any –

VERONICA. I'll change later, ok?

MATT. I was just –

VERONICA. It's your mom's shirt, not yours. Why do you care?

MATT. I…don't.

VERONICA. I like your mom.

MATT. She's all right.

VERONICA. Don't you like her?

MATT. She's my mom.

VERONICA. Yeah. And?

MATT. I mean, you're not really supposed to *like* your mom, are you? I mean, it's not – whatever.

VERONICA. What?

MATT. Do *you* like *your* mom?

VERONICA. Yeah. I love my mom. I really – I mean, sometimes I hate her so much, for – well. But you know, that's just because I –

(Her voice breaks, she pauses, catches her breath.)

… so much.

MATT. Wow.

VERONICA. What?

MATT. I…never heard anyone say that before. It's not very cool.

VERONICA. Yeah, well, I guess I'm not very –

MATT. No, no, you ARE, that's just the thing. I – nothing.

VERONICA. You always do that.

MATT. What?

VERONICA. Get just to the point of what you were going to say, and then say, "nothing" or "whatever." I mean, what's the point?

MATT. What point?

VERONICA. Yeah.

MATT. I don't – I forgot, what I was saying.

VERONICA. That I'm very cool.

MATT. Oh, right.

VERONICA. And – ?

MATT. Uh, that was all.

VERONICA. Thank you. By the way… Huey Lewis? Sucks.

MATT. What?

VERONICA. If you tell anyone I knew the words, I'm gonna have to kill you.

(pause)

Joke.

(He laughs, flustered.)

Sorta. You've got to check out Blondie. Everything…I don't know what it is…turns to color when you listen to her. Here. Now, *she…*

(She unplugs his headphones and plugs them into her Walkman. Presses "play.")

(She mouths the word to him:)

Rocks.

*(**MATT** listens to the music.)*

(A Blondie song from the 1980s, something like "One Way or Another" plays.*)

*(**VERONICA** watches him listen to her music.)*

---

* Please see Music Use Note on page 3.

Scene Five

AUROCH. *(reading)* "It is known that Laplanders herded and milked reindeer eleven thousand years ago. Thirty thousand years ago, people in the High Sinai were confining and breeding antelope with the aid of fences, an invention arguably as important as the spear..."

(She looks up and gazes over the fence, and stays watching as the scene begins.)

(Lights shift from fence, to:)

*(**MEG** sits on the porch steps, shucking corn.)*

*(**JAMES** enters.)*

JAMES. Quite a view. Mind if I – ?

(He sits down next to her.)

Sorry about the other night. I – don't know what came over me.

(She doesn't answer.)

You're just...such a good mom.

(She looks at him skeptically. He tries again.)

I guess I'm only human.

(She gives him an even more skeptical look.)

You don't like me very much, do you?

MEG. Is it in the contract that I have to?

JAMES. Didn't you read it?

(She looks at him uneasily, pause; he laughs, as if he were joking.)

You know, I'm actually very likeable.

MEG. Are you?

JAMES. I really am. You should give me a chance.

MEG. And why should I do that?

JAMES. Oh, I don't know. You might...like me?

(**MEG** *laughs a little, involuntarily.*)

MEG. Likeable…I just don't see it.

JAMES. I am. I really am. I mean, I'm a ball breaker in business, but in my personal life – well, "affable" is what they call me. "Relentlessly affable," I've even been called that.

MEG. It doesn't sound like a compliment.

JAMES. It means –

MEG. "Likeable." I know. "Without relent." I went to college.

JAMES. You did?

MEG. When the car drives by, the cows get down on all fours. But otherwise, they stand on two feet and drink cocktails like the city people.

JAMES. *(deadpan)* They *do?*

MEG. No, it's a – Oh, never mind.

(**AUROCH** *exits.*)

(**MEG** *and* **JAMES** *stare out at the view together.*)

JAMES. Sure is pretty out there.

MEG. Yeah.

JAMES. God's country.

MEG. I suppose you consider that a challenge.

JAMES. I think you overestimate me.

MEG. Never underestimate your enemy.

JAMES. How did I become that?

MEG. When you look out there, what do you see?

JAMES. I don't know. The same things you see…

MEG. I wouldn't assume that.

JAMES. Grass…hills. The way they go on and on, one into the next – No factories. No complications. No reminders. Like if I look at it long enough, my mind will be that, too. Peaceful, you know?

(He laughs.)

Kind of like a lobotomy.

MEG. See that silo over there?

JAMES. Where?

MEG. Right...near that...where those two hills...near that kind of ugly angular house...

(With her hands, she indicates a valley.)

JAMES. There are a lot of... Oh, okay. That's a nice house. Those hills. Sure. I see it.

MEG. Remember that spot. And now, over there, do you see that silo? Find that lake, then trace a line over to... there. Do you know how far apart those are?

JAMES. That's not fair, you've probably measured –

MEG. I don't need to. The answer's 1.5 miles. Now take that distance, and move your fingers...there...and you find another silo. Try it.

(He locks his fingers to the distance and moves one point to another spot, as with a drafting compass. They both search for a silo, that isn't there.)

Well, unless they've been destroyed. Here, try it going east.

(They try another way, simultaneously. It works.)

There. Used to be grist mills, too – precisely placed so that farmers could get there and pick up, and still get back in time for their evening milking. Same with the churches. All the buildings speckling the landscape. The whole design. Bare hills, fences... The whole landscape...made around the necessities of farming. A reason for every little detail out there. When I say "pretty"? That's what I see. Tongue in groove perfection.

JAMES. Cool little trick. It does hearken back to an era, doesn't it?

MEG. It's still a dairy landscape.

JAMES. Sure it is. And with trucks, you really have to worry about getting home from the silo in time. And church – !

MEG. What's that supposed to mean?

JAMES. It's quaint – anti*quaint*ed. Ha, that's a good one –
you can sell that.

MEG. I think I already did.

(beat)

JAMES. Let me help.

(He reaches for a piece of corn. She jerks it away.)

MEG. I've got it.

(Pause. She feels bad, relents a little.)

It's been dry. But there's still a few kernels. It's cattle
corn. But when it's young – it's not bad, eating. All
corn's gonna be tough this year.

JAMES. You know, I'd really like to help.

MEG. I told you, I've got it.

JAMES. No, I mean – *Matt.* I was thinking, maybe I could
arrange for an internship for him. Bring him to the
city, take him under my wing, train him –

MEG. To be like you?

JAMES. To get the things he wants.

MEG. I can take care of Matt just fine, thanks.

JAMES. Yeah, I've noticed.

MEG. I thought your kids were here to learn from us.

JAMES. It strikes me that we each have something they
could learn.

MEG. I wouldn't know. Where are they, your family?

JAMES. You really love this place, don't you?

MEG. Don't change the subject.

JAMES. My wife travels. She's big on charities. What about
you?

MEG. I can't afford charities.

JAMES. No, I mean – You went to college. For what?
Farming?

MEG. Mathematics. Tell me about your boys.

JAMES. She brings them with her. Well, the baby. The older one, John, he's…away…college. He's…a real achiever, that one! Mathematics?

MEG. My Jenny's in college.

JAMES. What did you want to be?

MEG. A mathematician, what do you think?

JAMES. So…what, you could micro-manage the farm?

MEG. She wants to be an actress. Her father doesn't approve, thinks it –

JAMES. I asked about you.

MEG. It didn't have anything to do with the farm.

JAMES. It's got a magnet this place, doesn't it.

MEG. Yeah. You could call it that.

(*beat*)

I was *out there*, for a while. Really doing it. Math. I was in grad school –

JAMES. Grad school's tough. I understand –

MEG. No, grad school – was fine, I loved it. I mean, it was *hard*, but…

JAMES. I know. I couldn't do it. Pure mathematics? Too much theory. I was an Econ major. More applied.

MEG. That's not the point. Mathematics is an art. Of seeing beyond the surface. Of capturing things no one else can see.

(*Pause. She looks out at the landscape.*)

Anyhow. Mom took sick. I came home, to take care of her. And Dad. He was an ace at the farm, but couldn't boil an egg. I was afraid he'd never eat anything but raw milk. Which, don't get me wrong, you can live on for a while, particularly when it's unpasteurized and unhomogenized, but – So two years into school, I came back, on a leave of absence. That spring, Mom died, I went to the feed store to pick up something for Dad, and…well, I met Ben. End of story.

JAMES. Funny. That's usually where the story begins.

MEG. Oh. Well, then, end of one story. Beginning of another.

JAMES. He worked there?

MEG. GOD no. He was a reporter – "journalist." He was wearing this stiff brand new unisuit and asking for a "claw" – that's the rubber teats that attach to a milking machine. Anyhow – He was "undercover." Doing a piece on the "back to the land" movement. Wanted to get the real first-hand perspective, wanted people to think he was a "native."

He stuck out like a sore thumb. I helped him. It made me feel good. I was so used to feeling like I was wasting my life here, to have him look at me like that, with that enthusiasm, like...like I held all the secrets he ever wanted to know...

JAMES. He fell for his subject. Very unprofessional.

MEG. *(She smiles, nostalgically.)* Yeah.

JAMES. He's not from around here then.

MEG. Ben? A city boy from the Bronx?

JAMES. Oh.

MEG. Not what you bargained for, is it?

JAMES. I never bargain.

MEG. *(digging at him)* "Authenticity" and all...

JAMES. I'm just patient. By the time I toss a deal out on that table, I'm fairly confident it can't be turned down. It's an acquired skill.

MEG. And you wonder why people don't like you.

JAMES. Not people, just you.

MEG. Why does it matter to you?

JAMES. I don't like it when you look at me that way.

MEG. What way?

JAMES. *That* way.

MEG. Then maybe you should try changing.

JAMES. Why do you think I came here?

MEG. To ruin my life?

(pause)

Why *did* you come here?

JAMES. I don't know, I guess what I do, wears on you after a while.

MEG. What do you do?

JAMES. You don't have to be polite.

MEG. I'm not.

JAMES. I'll bore you.

MEG. I'll tell you when to stop.

JAMES. *(chuckles)* Okay. Deal. I scout resources, for a corporation...a big guy. I have an "eye" – always have. I look for things...perfect things...something that has... I don't know, a certain vibrancy. Life. I find it. I recommend it. And we acquire it.

MEG. *Buy* it.

JAMES. Right. And then we "fix" it – modifications, improvements. We strip it of everything that doesn't produce. All the fat. And for one year, that baby produces like nobody's ever seen. All its reserves, burned up. I guess you can say I help it reach its true potential.

MEG. Then what?

JAMES. Oh, well, "then what"...not our business, "then what." We sell, while it's running strong.

MEG. Don't you ever –

JAMES. Look back? At what, my "legacy"? Listen, you can't think too much in this life. Better to look forward. I didn't make the system. The numbers are good. That's what matters. My Family. First and foremost. They need things.

MEG. It's not exactly a model of sustainability.

JAMES. It sustains *us*.

(He indicates around them.)

And this is?

MEG. It used to be.

JAMES. Except now you need me –

MEG. I don't, I – Okay, you can stop now.

JAMES. And everything I do, to keep you going.

MEG. I said *stop.* We made a deal –

JAMES. The farm needs me, and you need the farm.

MEG. I don't need the farm. I don't *need* anything.

JAMES. There it is again.

MEG. What?

JAMES. That look.

> *(pause)*

> Listen, I have a talent. I know it sounds hokey, but: Everything I touch? Turns to gold. I can't help it. The guys at the office, they used to kid me about it: "King Midas!" It was a joke. Kind of. But after a while, I couldn't stop. Everything I touched – *everything.* Gold is dead. That's why I came here. Suddenly I looked around me, and everything was – And I remembered this place. So clearly.

> *(He indicates the view.)*

MEG. *(softly)* Why didn't you stop? When I asked you to.

> *(He touches her wrist. She lets him.)*

JAMES. I can't.

> *(beat)*

> *(The fence:* **AUROCH** *appears on the far side.)*

AUROCH. Chapter 3: "As you can see, fencing has a role both in keeping animals in…and in keeping predators out."

> *(Long, low, prescient moo.)*

> *(Lights shift, to a late-night netherworld.)*

> *(***AUROCH*** *is immersed in the book.)*

> *(***MEG*** *steps up to her own side of the fence.)*

MEG. Can I help you?

AUROCH. No.

MEG. What are you doing?

AUROCH. Reading.

MEG. No, I mean…here. You're on private property.

AUROCH. Am I? I was just hiking…you know, the Appa-lachian.

MEG. That's over there.

(**AUROCH** *looks up from her book, and gives* **MEG** *her full and pointed attention.*)

AUROCH. Oh. I guess I lost my way…*strayed from the path.*

MEG. Where's your pack?

AUROCH. I travel alone.

MEG. No, I – meant your *bag.*

AUROCH. I don't carry any of those. If you live right, you don't have to. Know what I mean?

MEG. Should I know you?

AUROCH. I don't know, should you?

MEG. Where did you get that book?

AUROCH. Under his pillow, when he's sleeping. I take it.

MEG. Can I – ?

AUROCH. *Tsk tsk,* I have a code of morals, too, you know. I only steal for myself. You want it, you steal it. Or ask him. You don't even recognize me, do you?

MEG. Should I?

AUROCH. An egg divided in the wood. And I? I became the one less traveled by. Which did you become?

MEG. Is that supposed to be some kind of riddle?

AUROCH. You still have one, you know, *Sister.*

(**MEG** *regards her unkempt demeanor.*)

MEG. *(disappointed)* Oh, you're a feminist.

AUROCH. A what?

(*pause*)

Auroch, pleased to meet you.

(**AUROCH** *holds out her hand, to shake. It is, oddly, hooved.* **MEG** *stares at it, but doesn't accept it. She can't deal.*)

(**AUROCH** *retracts her hoof.*)

AUROCH. *(cont.)* Ooo-kay. We can always just...talk about the weather.

(awkward pause)

MEG. Some drought we got goin' here, huh?

AUROCH. It's gonna rain...big time.

MEG. I'll believe it when I see it.

AUROCH. You should try believing first. You might be surprised what you can see.

MEG. We haven't had a drop in months.

AUROCH. It will this time. I feel it, in my hide.

MEG. But the weatherman said...

AUROCH. He's gotten complacent, scared. Lost his knack. Afraid of being wrong. When it comes to weather? Never doubt a wild thing. It's going to rain torrents.

(They stare at the clouds.)

AUROCH. The earth's not ready for it.

(Pause. They lean on the fence, looking up at the same sky.)

(Surreptitiously, MEG reaches out her hand.)

AUROCH. Go on. I won't scurry away.

(MEG touches her skin. It's real.)

(Lights fade on MEG.)

Scene Six

AUROCH. *(reading James's book)* "Any cow I have ever owned has quickly gained control of her letdown reflex and, knowing the calf is waiting, will not let me have any milk. You may have to fight for your share of the milk, or be very clever, tactful or gifted at subterfuge... to get it."

(MEG and VERONICA are in the kitchen, making cheese together.)

MEG. Cheese-making is an old, old art. You know, I used to do it with my mom –

VERONICA. You're not that old.

MEG. No, I – that's not what I meant.

VERONICA. Oh, sorry, I –

MEG. I'm boring you.

VERONICA. No, I – I've never done anything so interesting. I mean, I – I really want to know.

MEG. It's like canning. Before we started messing with nature, cows only gave birth in the spring. There was fresh milk while the calves nursed, but – it was finite. Like a season. So they had to find a way to make it last, year round, into the winter. It's pragmatic, a pragmatic food, cheese is.

VERONICA. So you take some mold –

MEG. Culture. "Mesophilic culture." Sounds like one of the stone ages, doesn't it?

VERONICA. And add it to the fresh milk –

MEG. Basically. And rennet.

VERONICA. And –

MEG. Heat it.

VERONICA. Like this.

MEG. Till it reaches 96 degrees, slowly, over a half hour. That's your job, to watch it.

VERONICA. All my jobs are watching.

MEG. Best way to learn. Like listening before you talk.

VERONICA. Can I ask you something?

MEG. Sure.

VERONICA. Have you ever...seen a mink?

MEG. As in the creature or the coat?

VERONICA. The...animal.

MEG. Tons. Used to be a mink farm right down the road – old Shannahan farm. A few years back, some activists broke in, "freed" them, all those little minks, just... slipped out, "escaped," they didn't know why. Kind of like osmosis, I guess; more room out there – why not? – Into the wilderness. Five thousand hand-raised, bottle-fed minks. You know what that looks like? The roads were splattered for months. People died. A family over on Hollow Lane? Skidded out one night and – Between that and the foxes...Hundreds of them crept back into the farm after a while...But they were all beat up by then, their fur – useless. Had to be exterminated. Housing development's there now. Shannahan moved to Florida. Lasted about six months before his heart gave out, but. Well. I suppose some must have made it out there – minks...bred with wild ones, learned to be wild...Why'd you ask?

VERONICA. Oh. Uh, nothing.

MEG. "Free The Minks!" I guess it *seemed* like a good idea at the [time] – Hey, how we doing on *time?*

VERONICA. I wasn't –

MEG. You've got to keep your eye on it. Watching is an important job. Okay? Now, let's see.... Temperature's up to 65... Luckily, I saw the clock when we started... it's heating a little too fast, it'll ball up like rubber, we've got to...

(**MATT** *enters, all spiffed out in his new clothes: IZOD, chinos and Stan Smiths.*)

MATT. Hey.

MEG. Hi honey.

(She puts out her cheek to be kissed; he doesn't. She tries to ignore this, continues with her cheese making.)

VERONICA. Hey.

MATT. *(sheepishly)* Hey.

MEG. Where have you been? Your dad was looking for you. Why don't you go make yourself useful?

MATT. I might get dirty.

MEG. Life's dirty. Go help your father.

MATT. Veronica's dad said I didn't have to. I've got a job now. I don't need to help out anymore.

MEG. He said, *what?*

MATT. A job. Isn't that great? At Friendly's, scooping ice cream. I mean, it's not the best job, but – "There is no small job," that's what he said. Minimum wage for now, but that's more than I'm getting –

MEG. *Friendly's?*

MATT. It may just seem like a family restaurant, but really it's structured just like any corporation.

MEG. You're more valuable to us here than any minimum wage –

MATT. They pay me.

MEG. Well, you – we –

MATT. There's room to grow.

MEG. I said – go help your father. We'll talk about this later.

MATT. But I might get my clothes dirty.

MEG. So, we'll wash them.

MATT. I don't know how to get sour milk off an *IZOD*…do you?

MEG. What?

(She finally turns and looks at him.)

White sneakers?

MATT. Stan Smiths. Check it out.

MEG. Where did you get those?

*(**JAMES** enters.)*

MATT. Oh, hey! What do you think? Do they fit ok?

JAMES. Like they were made for you.

MATT. Aren't they a little…?

(He indicates the rear, which is perfectly baggy.)

JAMES. They're supposed to fit that way. Trust me. I consulted with experts.

VERONICA. He's not kidding. He does, consult with…

MEG. *Trust* you?

MATT. Cool.

(MEG takes her hands out of the cheese, and wipes them on her pants. She's about to touch MATT's shirt. He flinches. She looks at him.)

MATT. Sorry, it's just – they're a little…you know, dirty.

MEG. I wasn't going to touch the shirt. I was just – there's a loose thread.

JAMES. That's not possible.

MEG. I was going to pluck it.

JAMES. That shirt was hand-checked and –

MEG. Oh, my mistake. You're right.

JAMES. – tailored by my personal –

MEG. It's not loose at all. It leads right back to you.

MATT. Mom, you are so weird.

MEG. Nice fit, too bad you have to give them back.

MATT. What?

JAMES. It's a gift to him, not you –

MATT. He's just trying to be *nice*, Mom.

MEG. *Nice?*

MATT. It's between him and me. Our thing. Not yours, okay? Everything to do with me isn't your – Can't you just let him be *nice?*

(Beat. He looks at her with hatred. She flinches.)

MEG. Okay. Keep them. Fine. But go change, *now*, and help your father.

(He looks beseechingly at **JAMES**.*)*

JAMES. I can't tell you what to do. But I would recommend you change your shoes. You've got replacements for the others.

MEG. Replacements?

MATT. The shirts. Six of them, identical, in different colors. It's like a rainbow. But, uh, you know, cooler.

(She contains her anger. He sees he's tested her enough, and, carefully, leaves.)

*(***VERONICA** *is clearly agitated.)*

VERONICA. I'll go.

MEG. You have a job. You watch the cheese.

*(***VERONICA** *puts on her Walkman and withdraws into herself.* **MEG** *and* **JAMES** *are virtually left alone.)*

MEG. What are you doing?

JAMES. He's right, I'm just being nice, I – I wanted to do something nice for you.

MEG. Now, why would you want to do that.

JAMES. I don't know what you want. So, I figured, well, I know what *he* wants. She wants him to be happy. I can make him happy. It's nothing to me –

MEG. Oh, but it's something to him.

JAMES. Which is why I'm doing it.

MEG. Which is why you're doing it.

JAMES. You can disagree with me at any moment.

MEG. Oh, no, I agree completely.

(pause)

Matt wants things. It's weak, but he does.

JAMES. We all do. It's natural.

MEG. And sometimes nature needs to be controlled. Responsible farming. A little cultivation –

JAMES. I'm talking about people.

MEG. So am I.

(He kisses her.)

(What she feels surprises her. She has to fight it.)

MEG. What are you trying to do to us?

JAMES. I don't know… Help you?

MEG. You can't buy us, not our…affection. We've been around a long time. That's what I love about my family. We're made of stronger stuff than that.

*(Beat. **BEN** bursts in.)*

BEN. Helloooo, Mr. Kubota.

MEG. Kubota?

JAMES. You like it.

BEN. Like it? LIKE it – ?! Meg, you've got to try this out.

MEG. Kubota, as in…

BEN. The finest piece of farm equipment you've ever –

MEG. *(her heart in her throat)* That…tractor you've always wanted?

BEN. Oh, no, not "that tractor." Not just "a" "tractor" –

JAMES. I thought if we were really serious about getting things done on this place –

BEN. A piece of *machinery*.

JAMES. Then we'd better get some serious –

BEN. You've never seen anything like this.

JAMES. Equipment.

MEG. IZODs. Stan Smiths. A new tractor.

JAMES. I hope you don't feel left out.

BEN. I'm telling you Meg, it's not a tractor, it's – a steel arm, is what it is. I mean, you sit there, way up in that tall seat, and you look out…the landscape…spread out before you. And find something that needs to be moved. Anything. I'm telling you, the biggest fucking boulder you have ever –

MEG. We don't have boulders, Ben.

VERONICA. Um, Mrs. –

BEN. Sure we do. These fields are built on boulders.

MEG. But there's no need to remove them. We work around them. We always have –

BEN. But now we *can*. All you do is, you set your eyes on it. It's deep in the soil, baked clay, whatever's out there. And you stare at it. Then you lift your hand, slightly, you reach out, and you grip that lever. And then: you move it. And sure enough, you get right in there. No separation. You just dig in and tear that motherfucker out. I am indomitable. I am steel, these arms are – c'mon baby, let me bring you for a ride.

(He grabs her and tries to lift her, pinches his back.)

Ouch. Shit.

*(**MEG** tries to help him. He brushes her off, tries to regain his edge.)*

*(to **JAMES**)*

You're a good guy, do you know that? I wasn't sure at first, I have to say, I was skeptical – Wasn't I skeptical, honey?

*(**MEG** gives **BEN** a skeptical look.)*

But *now*....

*(bent over a little, to **MEG**)*

You want a ride?

MEG. Later. I have to finish the cheese.

BEN. Who wants to know what it feels like to be a man?

*(**VERONICA** raises her hand, shyly, trying to get **MEG**'s attention.)*

I was actually…looking for Matt.

VERONICA. Mrs. –

MEG. Matt's not going to be helping you anymore. He has a job.

BEN. He sure does. Out in the new barn.

MEG. It's at Friendly's.

BEN. What the hell is he doing at Friendly's?

MEG. It…may seem like just a family restaurant, but really it…it's structured like any other corporation.

JAMES. Nicely done.

(beat)

MEG. What new barn, Ben?

BEN. Oh, we…wanted to surprise you. It's almost finished, up in the west pasture. We had one of those modules hauled in while you were out getting supplies over in Fayetteville. But it was a bitch with the old tractor, your dad's, you know – antiquated stuff. Take days to put a barn up. But now – Now we can almost lift the whole thing with one –

(She grabs his arm.)

MEG. What "whole thing?"

BEN. You make the cheese, honey. We'll take care of it.

MEG. "We'll take care of it"? "You make the cheese"?! I demand to know what you're –

BEN. For the Highlands. You know, the bulls.

VERONICA. I was trying to tell you…it…it got too warm, it…

MEG. Since when do decisions get made here without me? Since when has anything new been added on here that I don't know about? I mean, whose farm *is* this anyhow?!

(Beat. They all look…awkward. The answer is clear.)

*(**VERONICA** has her headset on.)*

(She yells over what she thinks is them talking.)

VERONICA. It's ruined. I always fuck things up. I ruin everything, I'M SORRY, I –

(She realizes she is yelling into the silence. She presses "stop" on her Walkman.)

(quietly)

I didn't know what to do.

(The lights fade on the kitchen.)

(**AUROCH** *is at the fence.* **MEG** *steps into the night.*)

MEG. What's it like?

AUROCH. What?

MEG. You know, out…there.

AUROCH. In this day and age? Not easy, let me tell you. Scurrying between the patches of green – Darting through housing developments – zigging, zagging, leaping blindly across paved roads – But you've got to keep roaming, roam or die. When they start to squeeze you out, fence you in, I mean…what are the options?

MEG. Don't look at me like that.

AUROCH. Like what?

MEG. You're a…a *cow*, right? Where are your nice, wide-set, all-accepting *cow* eyes?

AUROCH. That's not acceptance, that's in-breeding.

(pause)

I think I know what you need.

MEG. Some gin?

AUROCH. To moo.

MEG. To *what*?

AUROCH. You know how to moo, don't you?

(doing her best Bacall)

You just put your lips together…and bellow.

(**AUROCH** *cracks herself up.*)

MEG. Oh, great. An auroch with a sense of humor.

(**AUROCH**'s *laughter gets a little wild, with snorts, wilderness wild. Then suddenly she stops and becomes very still.*)

AUROCH. *(serious)* How do you think I survived so long?

(lights)

(INTERIOR: **BEN***)*

(The distant sound of cows bellowing.)

(BEN enters with a big boom box, looking out to the field.)

(He gazes out at the view.)

(He checks his watch, a pregnant pause; then presses "play.")

(A Puccini aria ["Nessun Dorma"] blares, as if out of his chest.)

(Distant cow bells, rhythmic, paced, get closer and closer, until:)

(The bells are as close as the music.)

(He smiles, turns down the music, and the encroaching cowbells take over.)

BEN. That's it – c'mon. Time to eat.

End of Act 1

ACT 2

Scene One

(A week later. The sound of torrential rain. The distant sounds of cowbells clanking. Soft, slightly desperate mooing of many cows and bulls, dull thuds of their bodies against steel walls.)

AUROCH. "The period of greatest heat activity is between twelve midnight and six a.m. If she has a bell on, you will hear a great deal of ringing."

(The sounds increase. They will build momentum over the scene.)

*(Lights down on **AUROCH**, up on kitchen.)*

BEN. Jesus Christ, this goddam rain. Try the radio.

MEG. When it rains it pours!

*(**BEN** glares at her.)*

It's broken. Remember? The dial. From last time, when you tried to – To NPR.

BEN. Goddam –

MEG. Well, they have local news sometimes, I mean, especially at a time like –

VOICE OF COMMENTATOR. And what better time is there, to show your support –

BEN. Jesus Christ, it's a fund drive.

MEG. Ohh-kay. So we shut it off.

BEN. I can't now. The switch –

VOICE OF COMMENTATOR. Call in now, and get an NPR tote bag! AND your special subscription to our free weekly program guide. For just a twenty-five dollar pledge. That breaks down to –

MEG. Oh, wait, let me get my checkbook – I'll call.

BEN. The phone is dead.

MEG. Humor, Ben. It goes a long way –

BEN. A *little bit* goes a long way –

MEG. I wasn't actually going to –

BEN. More than that? –

VOICE OF COMMENTATOR. Right now is a *particularly* good time to join WAMC…

BEN. – Aggressive.

VOICE OF COMMENTATOR. And now, let us listen to our theme song, the lovely Kate Smith, singing "God Bless America"…

(Kate Smith comes on, in her tinny voice, underscoring the rest of the scene.)*

(The lights flicker.)

BEN. Oh, great. Not again.

(The lights go out, again.)

Shit.

(The stage is dark, nothing. Tension in the darkness.)

(Kate Smith continues to sing.)

*(**MEG** fumbles in the dark, lights a match.)*

MEG. Matches. Lantern. Voila! I'm getting so good at this I could do it in the dark.

(She lights the kerosene lantern. The room jumps to a ghostly white life.)

BEN. *(deadpan)* You're on fire tonight, aren't you.

MEG. *(ignoring him, satisfied)* There…

BEN. Where's Matt?

MEG. In his room. You should know.

BEN. He could help out here a little bit.

MEG. Which is it – lock-down or help-out? You can't have both.

---

* Please See Music Use Note on Page 3.

BEN. You think I was too hard on him.

(She doesn't answer.)

He was caught buying DRUGS, for God's sake, Meg, DRUGS –

MEG. Not drugs, sugar pills –

BEN. Yeah, well, he *thought* they were drugs.

MEG. I know, I feel so bad for him…

BEN. MEG!

MEG. It's so…embarrassing.

BEN. Our son was hauled out of school –

MEG. I mean, if you're going to do it –

BEN. By the POLICE –

MEG. You might as well, you know….

BEN. – and all you can say is –

MEG. *Do* it. You know?

BEN. It's gonna be hell for business.

MEG. Is that all you can – ?

BEN. We have to maintain a certain *aura*, a certain wholesome –

MEG. People don't give a damn about the drugs, Ben. As long as our cows aren't taking them.

BEN. Oh, *that*'s naïve –

MEG. *You* act like we still rely on customers.

(beat)

The farm, the cows, milk – What about Matt? Don't you ever think about him?

BEN. Oh, I have a whole list of things for Matt, don't you worry. We'll start with the barn. One shovel at a time, *in* his goddam white sneakers. That will teach him a –

MEG. Great, another lesson. That's exactly what he needs.

(pause)

He wants things, Ben.

BEN. Obviously.

MEG. Did you ever ask him?

(He tinkers with the radio, more and more frustrated.)

BEN. This thing is going to drive me –

(to **MEG***)*

Wants are not to be trusted.

MEG. Did you ever think to –

BEN. Oh, so now it's my fault?

MEG. It's no one's fault, I'm just saying –

BEN. He could never afford to buy drugs –

(to the radio)

I've got to shut this goddam thing –

MEG. Sugar pills –

BEN. – before he started that job. Is what I'm saying.

(He hits the radio on the table's edge. The batteries fall out. It is finally silent. He looks at it, satisfied.)

There.

MEG. Yeah, well, well whose fault is that?

*(***JAMES*** enters in his pajamas. They are perfectly pressed.)*

JAMES. Jesus Christ, what a ruckus.

*(***MEG*** glares at him. ***BEN*** turns away, embarrassed.)*

Not you – the cows. They're driving me insane. Can't you quiet them down?

MEG. And how do you propose that?

JAMES. I don't know, don't you have…bovine *tranquilizers*, or something?

MEG. Oh, sure, give them *drugs*, that's a brilliant idea. Ben and I were just talking about that, weren't we, Ben?

*(***BEN*** shrinks from the conversation.)*

JAMES. Hey, it's not my fault that he bought…sugar pills.

(He laughs – he can't help it, he thinks this is incredibly funny.)

MEG. Don't mock him.

JAMES. I'm not, it's just – I mean, if you're going to *do* it –

MEG. Yeah, well, he thought he was, okay?

BEN. Meg, what are you saying?

MEG. Someone's got to speak up for him.

(The cows get really loud.)

JAMES. Can't you…stifle them, somehow?

MEG. What about your bulls? Can't you?

JAMES. My bulls aren't the ones in heat.

MEG. Oh, like the girls can control that?

BEN. *(desperately)* Let's talk about the weather.

MEG. Oh, no, I think we should talk about where he got the money.

JAMES. I showed him how to get it. He already had the impulse.

MEG. He couldn't act on it.

JAMES. That's not being "good" – that's called "lack of opportunity."

MEG. We all have desires. But we don't just go around… *acting* on them.

JAMES. I don't know, maybe we should.

(tense moment between them)

BEN. We do? Like what?

MEG. *(flustered)* I mean – That's what makes the world a civil place…right?

JAMES. What, repression?

(off-hand, like it's so obvious it bores him)

Listen, civilization is made by choice. If you can't afford options, you're not *choosing* the right path, you're just following it. Without choice, you're no one: a blank slate, undefined. That's what differentiates us from… animals.

(He gestures to the sound of the cows.)

(His and MEG's eyes meet again.)

(beat)

MEG. I thought you were an Econ major. What's with the philosophy?

JAMES. I dabbled. The point is, you should be happy. He's making choices.

BEN. Like getting hauled out of Woodshop in handcuffs?

JAMES. *(chuckling)* I bet *that* gets him a couple of dates.

BEN. Can't you be serious? He's my son –

JAMES. He's becoming someone.

> *(A sheet of rain hits the side of the house and breaks a window.)*

> *(Water streams in. The sounds get louder.)*

BEN. Oh, shit.

> *(He scrambles to patch it.)*

> *(yelling over the din, from the corner)*

What happened to the days of slow, steady rains? Can you tell me that?

JAMES. *(yelling back)* It's only going to get worse.

BEN. What?

JAMES. The gaps. The pendulum. It's – something global. Just...what I've heard.

> *(**JAMES** is peering out another window, towards the barn.)*

> *(**MEG** drifts over to him.)*

> *(The bellowing gets really intense for a while, then subsides.)*

MEG. Nothing like the peaceful country, huh?

JAMES. *(trying to ignore her)* I get the bellowing, but what's that thudding?

MEG. Their bodies, ramming up against the metal walls...

JAMES. Oh.

MEG. ...of your new barn.

JAMES. Shit.

MEG. Which property damage are you concerned about, your barn or your bulls?

JAMES. My sanity.

MEG. I don't know, it sounds kind of wild to me.

JAMES. Yeah, well –

MEG. Cows, bulls… "I thought you were a modern man, Ben?"

JAMES. I get your point.

MEG. "What are you, a Romantic?"

(They look at each other: a combo of conflict, hate, admiration and attraction.)

BEN. Meg!

(trying to distract her)

I need a hand here.

MEG. We signed a contract, Ben, not an oath of silence.

(a surge of moos)

JAMES. That's it.

MEG. Be careful what you wish for. Is all I'm saying.

JAMES: Where are you going?

JAMES. I'm going to town. Money can still buy you a little peace there, right? Stay at the Motor Inn, go to the pub, sit in the car, and listen to the radio, I don't care, anything but – *this.*

(He prepares to go, gets all the way to the door.)

BEN. *(quietly)* You – can't.

JAMES. Nobody tells me –

BEN. No, I mean…it's not *possible.*

*(**JAMES** glares at him.)*

The road, it's – At the bottom of the hill where it –

MEG. The road to town –

BEN. It's the only road. It's – wiped out.

(pause)

JAMES. I'll call my chopper. He'll be here in an hour.

(He picks up the phone. Listens. Taps the receiver. Nothing.)

Fuck.

BEN. I guess we're…just gonna have to wait it out.

JAMES. Well. We may not have enough tranquilizers for the cows, but there's only three of us. Now that's efficiency.

*(**JAMES** takes out a vial of pills.)*

BEN. How can you – ? And at a time like – ?

*(**JAMES** goes to the refrigerator.)*

JAMES. This fresh?

MEG. The one to the left is tonight's.

JAMES. It's still warm.

(He drinks out of the bottle.)

Let's get one thing straight. I didn't do anything. I got him a job, bought him some clothes. Most people would be goddam grateful. I just provide the means. Human nature takes care of itself.

(He tosses back some pills, is about to leave, then spills a few onto the table.)

Go on, knock yourselves out.

(He exits.)

*(**MEG** and **BEN** sit in silence together. The sound of the cows is deafening now, but they just sit there, still.)*

BEN. It helps if you just give into it.

MEG. Channel the vibrations?

BEN. Like we used to, remember, out in the barn?

MEG. That was just once. You'd think we were teenagers, the way you talk about it.

(They sit still. She smiles, begrudgingly.)

It does…help.

BEN. *(trying)* When was the last time you felt passion like that?

(He tries to touch her. Tense moment.)

MEG. Don't.

BEN. Well, I guess I'd better go out there and check on the cows.

MEG. Ben –

(He grabs his raingear, opens the door. The storm elements are louder. He exits into it, slamming the door behind him.)

(beat)

*(**JAMES** steps back into the room. He and **MEG** lock eyes. He steps closer. Touches her. They kiss. Tentatively, then with all the instinct of survival.)*

(They move onto the table. The mooing and crashing of cow bodies against metal walls, torrential rain, gets louder, deafening, until suddenly there is a loud and ominous crash.)

*(**MEG** and **JAMES** both sit straight upright in horror.)*

*(**BEN** rushes in with a couple of guns.)*

BEN. Meg! The barn gave out, the bulls, they're loose, they're mounting every fucking thing in –

(He sees them, catches his breath, becomes pale rigid and still.)

–sight.

(The bellowing is intense outside.)

(He gently places a gun down and turns.)

I could use a hand. When you're ready.

(He opens the door back into the intense weather and noise, and exits, leaving the door open.)

(Loud storm noises transition to:)

Scene Two

(Interior: Matt)

*(**MATT** is shoveling hay. He's trapped in teenage angst and frustration. It's all going into the pitchfork. He's wearing his Walkman. The sound of intense, wild drumming in his ears.)*

*(**VERONICA** comes by. He doesn't see her. She watches him quietly a moment, admiring him.)*

VERONICA. Hey. *(pause.)* HEY.

(She taps him. Lights shift:)

(Surprised, he swings the pitchfork around, she jumps back.)

MATT. What are you doing here?

VERONICA. I was just…watching the calf.

MATT. Why are you wasting your time doing that?

VERONICA. It's not wasting time, it's my *chore.* Your dad told me – Will you put that down? – your dad told me I have to keep an eye on her, make sure she's okay, ten minutes a day, just sit there – I told him, how will I know if something's wrong? That's a big responsibility, I don't – I'm no authority on calves.

MATT. You will be.

VERONICA. Yeah, that's what he said. Ten minutes a day, and –

MATT. I know. He told me that once, too.

VERONICA. She's so cute.

MATT. Yeah, I've raised one before. They're always –

VERONICA. You should watch her with me.

MATT. I've done that already. Okay?

(beat)

VERONICA. How are you?

MATT. Fine.

VERONICA. No, I mean…I heard about the –

MATT. Oh, yeah, that. He's my usual supplier. But this time –

VERONICA. I'm glad they were sugar pills.

MATT. It's usually really strong shit, it's usually –

VERONICA. I'm glad you didn't go to jail. I'm glad you didn't go away. I told you not to do them anymore.

MATT. I know, but.

VERONICA. You have to be firm with yourself. Try – I don't know, reading. Or.

MATT. Yeah.

VERONICA. Knitting. Start another habit, it's the only way, to kick it –

MATT. You're still wearing her shirt.

VERONICA. Don't change the subject. Promise.

MATT. What?

VERONICA. To stop.

MATT. OK. I promise. Now can I change the subject?

VERONICA. Sure.

MATT. You have two huge suitcases. Full – unless that's bricks in there, or money, or – Don't you have any shirts of your own?

VERONICA. Your mom hasn't asked for it back.

MATT. So?

VERONICA. Why does it bother you so much?

MATT. Your clothes are cool.

VERONICA. I guess. But – all my clothes are – My dad's secretary picked them all out. They're –

MATT. I like them. They're –

VERONICA. – perfect. Stiff. This is comfortable. I can get it dirty, I – look, here's milk, from the calf. Here's a grass stain, from where I was running and slipped, and – this here's from baking. And this one – okay, that's gross, I don't know what that's from, the chicken coop maybe but –

MATT. Why don't you just get a scrap book?

VERONICA. I like it, okay? Your mom, she's…comfortable, in her skin, you know? I like wearing her shirt. It… feels good.

MATT. Oh.

VERONICA. YOU can wear my clothes if you want. See how they feel on you.

MATT. Uh…

VERONICA. Joke.

MATT. *(awkward laugh)* Right.

VERONICA. Do you *want* to, wear them?

MATT. What do you think I am, *gay?*

VERONICA. No. But it's cool if you are. I mean, *personally* disappointing, but…

MATT. *(flustered)* Oh. uh.

VERONICA. …cool.

(Tense silence, a little dangerous, warm, uncertain; it could go anywhere.)

VERONICA. *(quietly)* Did you see them, the bodies?

MATT. The what?

VERONICA. Cows, bulls – Dad's Highlands. In the storm, they broke loose, they stampeded, they –

MATT. I know what happened

VERONICA. – had to "put them down." I heard gunshots. A lot of them.

MATT. That was the rain, on the tin barn.

VERONICA. Don't try to protect me. I know what it was.

MATT. Okay, whatever, they're – Beef cattle get slaughtered. You can't get attached.

VERONICA. I saw my dad, standing by them – the pile your dad made, with his new tractor? He was sobbing, my dad was. I've – never seen him cry before, not over anything, not over – I wanted to go over, I wanted to –

(pause)

But I went to the field instead. It's still there.

MATT. What is?

VERONICA. You know. The weasel – mink –

MATT. You are so twisted. Can't you talk about anything else?

VERONICA. I tried to keep away from it, I really did.

MATT. I really don't want to –

VERONICA. I guess I kind of thought it would pretty much look like it did the other day. I think I thought it would *always* look that way, you know? Smooth, peaceful. But… it changed. The fur's…not slick anymore. It's kind of… slimy. All of a sudden! And…there are three big holes, bored through its belly, they're kind of amazing, deep, round, perfect, like quarters.

MATT. I really don't want to hear this.

(He puts on his headset.)

VERONICA. And next to each one? A big fat beetle. I've never seen this kind before. They're nasty. They're big, and they've got these hard black shells, and – LISTEN. Where did they come from? You don't see these things flying around, or on a flower. They're heavy, they don't look like they can fly. They just – I mean, they must feed on flesh, you know, corpses. They must just… move on, from one, to the next, to…nomadic, you know? I mean, I guess there's never an end of corpses, is there? Rotting out there, decomposing –

MATT. Will you stop? All you can talk about is this stupid weasel –

VERONICA. Mink –

MATT. Mink then –

VERONICA. Weasel –

MATT. I don't want to think about it, okay?

VERONICA. I was going to bring a book over, you know – *Indigenous Creatures of North America* – to check, compare, but I guess it's too late now. It's features are –

MATT. Will you shut up? I don't want to know. You found that weasel –

VERONICA. – mink.

MATT. THING. You found it the day BC died. Did you ever think about that? Did you ever think for one minute how I might – ? I mean, you're so clinical about it. It's DEATH, Veronica – it's not just…it's not just the body that goes. Haven't you ever had anything you really care about die?

VERONICA. Yeah. My mom.

MATT. Oh.

(beat)

But I thought –

VERONICA. Yeah, charities. Causes. Travel. It's what my dad says so he doesn't have to talk about it. No one wants to talk about it. No one – it's why we came here. He doesn't know what to do with us, he thought, we're – too old for a nanny! That's for sure. My brother, Johnny? He's in Rehab, Arizona – is that a place? – and my other one, well, if you don't have the right nursery school, you'll never get into the right pre-K, so *he's* home with the nanny, and…so that leaves me. And him. And he – no one wants to talk about it.

MATT. Oh. I'm –

VERONICA. Don't be. It wasn't your fault. Just – listen. Can you do that?

(pause)

We used to go shopping together. It wasn't the stuff… it was the time together, alone, you know? Every thing we picked out for each other, it was like saying – I *know* you. I look at that, and I see you…. In this and this and – *it's who I think you are.* Who *I* think – She was so perfect. Smooth and shiny and the way she smelled – no one else smelled like her. She would leave sometimes, to go out, to a charity ball or something, and. I would slip into her robe, her shirt, whatever she was wearing before she left. It didn't make me feel like her. I could never be like *her*. But I felt her around me.

Warm. Holding me in. I kept some of her things, after she died? But, the smell wore out after a while, it just – got so…faint, you know? Those suitcases…most of it's hers.

(long pause)

MATT. Did you name the calf yet?

VERONICA. In my head, but I didn't want to – I mean, she's yours really. I'm just watching her.

MATT. No, she's yours, she – what's the name?

VERONICA. TL. Tiger Lily, I thought – like in *Peter Pan*? And those really pretty flowers that grow wild, bunched up against the fence.

(He smiles.)

MATT. Did you check her eyes, you know, they can get this infection –

VERONICA. Yeah, your dad told me.

(Pause. Something in her head makes her break into a grin.)

You know, the Greeks? They made up this word. To describe a sucking calf? *"Exuberance."* Did you know that? It's so great, I mean, it's so – PERFECT. "Exuberance." Just – Your mom told me that. She's one smart lady.

(Pause. She looks sideways at him, carefully.)

(tentatively)

I wonder what comes next – you know, after those beetles?

MATT. Yeah, I – I guess I do, too.

Scene Three

(**MEG** *is sitting on a 3-legged milking stool, milking a cow in the barn. She has a rocking rhythm going, as she expertly moves from one teat to the next. The sound of milk hitting a metal bucket synchs with her hands.* **JAMES** *enters, quietly, in the shadows. The lights begin to shift to "Interior":*)

(**MEG** *literally can't milk anymore. She looks up.*)

MEG. You might as well come out.

JAMES. How did you – ?

MEG. The milk – it dried up.

JAMES. You've got to be kidding me.

(**MEG** *looks at him; she doesn't look like she's kidding.*)

Classic sign of the devil, eh?

MEG. Yeah, well, it's not all fire and brimstone. What were you doing?

JAMES. Oh, just…reading.

MEG. In the dark?

JAMES. Watching. You. The sunlight, how it hits your hair, through the – the beams there, the slats in them. It's so…so… God, that *smell* –

MEG. It'll go away after a while.

JAMES. I can't get it out of my nostrils.

MEG. No cows, no cowshit –

JAMES. That's not what I –

MEG. No *bulls*, no – [bullshit]

JAMES. I meant the burning.

MEG. I warned you, didn't I? – Highlands are beef cattle. What you smell is the hair, and the hide. Without that, it's just a barbecue.

(*He looks a little nauseous.*)

That was a joke.

JAMES. About last night –

MEG. A natural disaster, okay? Or maybe an over-civilized one, I don't know. Forget it –

JAMES. I can't.

MEG. Give it time.

JAMES. How can you be so calm?

MEG. Electricity's still out. Cows have to be milked – one by one. It's my job. We have a responsibility to things we own. To take care of them. Not to put them in peril. Not to make stupid choices based on whimsy – Stop me if I'm telling you anything you already know – I have to be calm, to milk. To do my job. My part of the bargain. Life goes on –

JAMES. *Some* life –

MEG. Yes. *Some* life.

   (beat)

JAMES. Did you see them out there?

MEG. Are they all you can think about?

JAMES. They were –

MEG. Slipping, sliding, an avalanche of mud, fucking anything that stayed still long enough – I saw them. I saw your whole damn prefab barn go floating down the hill, too, tearing out everything in its path. What did you expect? What did you want from us? All these... unbridled instincts, all these – natural reactions in an unnatural environment.

JAMES. You killed them. You pulled the –

MEG. Trigger. Sure. *Mercy.* But you put us here.

   (beat)

JAMES. My beautiful Scottish Highlands...

MEG. We weren't meant for this.

JAMES. They looked so beautiful out there, out on the... *range,* they –

MEG. Will you stop this?

JAMES. Looked so free.

(pause)

Just this once, I wanted to *create* something, to put something out there that really *lived*.

MEG. What about your daughter?

JAMES. That's just it. I'm so afraid…

MEG. You never even look at her.

JAMES. …to look at her, touch her…

MEG. She's right there and –

JAMES. Of what will happen, of what she'll become, of what I'll –

MEG. So you leave her to herself, without anyone? To talk to, to –

JAMES. No, I bought her a whole farm, for God's sake. *I brought her here.*

(sadly)

I wanted it to be so different this time.

(Beat. The bottom drops out of their passion: for anger, revenge, anything.)

MEG. Here, I can't anymore. My hands are tired. You do it.

(She gets up and offers her seat.)

JAMES. Milk? I can't –

MEG. You like it so much. You might as well learn how to get it.

JAMES. But I'll – I mean, I can't, I'll – ruin it.

(He indicates touching the udder.)

MEG. It's too late to worry about that. Go on.

(Pause. He sits down, instantly almost falls off.)

(chuckles, despite herself)

Easy there. First thing to remember is, there's only three legs. Don't treat it like it's four. Just cause that's what you're used to. There's a reason for it –

(She positions the stool the right way under him.)

MEG. *(cont.)* Good. Now. Put your head against her belly. It steadies her, and you can hear her heart.

JAMES. Whoa, that doesn't sound like her heart.

MEG. She's got four bellies in there, chances are one of them is digesting at any given moment.

(She puts her hands over his, and tries to get some milk from a teat. Nothing.)

MEG. This isn't going to work.

JAMES. Give me a chance. I just started.

MEG. No, I mean – You've got to think...Positive thoughts.

JAMES. What?

MEG. Picture – I don't know, peaceful things.

JAMES. How can she –

MEG. She'll know. And she won't give it up. Trust me.

JAMES. You mean, I'm not the devil?

MEG. No, you're – just...a little too tense.

(He closes his eyes, tries to milk.)

You're not doing it. Take a breath.

(He tries again. She watches, skeptical. She gives up, turns her back to him. The sound of a shot of milk squirting into a metal pail.)

MEG. There...now you are. Aren't you.

JAMES. How did you know?

MEG. I didn't. She did.

JAMES. Oh.

(MEG crouches down and helps him for a minute, her hands squeezing over his. Then she lets go. He continues. The sound of milk hitting the metal pan with downright "exuberance." JAMES beams. MEG steps back and watches, a sad smile in her eyes.)

(Lights shift. Meg's speech is internal; James doesn't hear her.)

MEG. Milk, whole milk, in it's raw form? Purest thing in the world – all that good bacteria, all those enzymes. But then you boil it – *pasteurization* – kill off everything living, so it's sterile, clean. Next you skim off the cream – that sells for more. The rest you spin against itself – *homogenization* – no lumps, no fat, so you can pour it into one big vat and never have to stir. So it matches everyone else's. And then we expect to have the same thing we started with, but I don't know what, less… risky? More stabilized? So it lasts longer, so they can package it, ship it out, so it can survive out there in the world. We call it Whole Milk, but – how can you put anything through all that, and expect to have the same thing you started with? "Whole Milk," Jesus Christ –

(She chokes with feeling.)

Problem is, the pure stuff? It corrupts so easily…

(The milk stops flowing.)

(He tries to squeeze, but it's dry.)

JAMES. *(sadly)* Nothing.

MEG. You're tense again.

JAMES. …Not me.

*(Lights shift. **AUROCH** wanders on, muddy, with charcoal marks on her arms. She has been watching from the shadows. She reads.)*

AUROCH. "'Sacred cow.' The term, as it applies, comes to us from India. But travel changes things – migration, from one land to the next, adaptation, survival. In Hindi, the *authentic*, 'agh anya', it means…not 'God', not *religion*, but 'that which cannot be slaughtered,' the *one thing* – Anything."

(She closes the book.)

Just. Name it. And stick to it. Don't let it down.

*(On the steps, **MEG** pores though a cardboard box full of yellowed old papers.)*

(Lights up full to "normal" lighting. **AUROCH** *watches her, considers, takes a breath and walks through the fence into the farm yard for the first time.)*

AUROCH. *(cont.)* Hey. What are you doing?

MEG. Oh, just sorting through some old –

(double-takes)

Wait. What are you doing here?

AUROCH. I guess I have a way of cropping up.

(pause)

I came to say goodbye –

MEG. Goodbye?

AUROCH. The season's changing. It's time, to migrate, to… mooove on. New pastures. You can smell it, in the air, can't you smell it?

MEG. All I smell is burning cow hair.

AUROCH. That's temporary. If you were wild, you would –

MEG. Yeah, well, I guess I'm not wild, am I?

AUROCH. I've got to go.

*(**AUROCH** turns to go. The book is in her back pocket.)*

MEG. No wait, I – I'm sorry, I –

(seeing the book)

You stole his book again.

AUROCH. No. I'm going clean. I didn't have to – he tossed it.

*(She shows it to **MEG**.)*

MEG. *"Keeping A Family Cow"?*

AUROCH. It's just…a how-to book. It –

MEG. A *how-to* book? That's it? It –

AUROCH. – *didn't work.* I think he didn't read it all the way through. Just, you know – skimmed it, dog-eared the good parts.

*(Pause. She assesses **MEG**.)*

Don't be so hard on yourself.

MEG. I don't know what you're –

AUROCH. What did you expect?

(*pointedly*)

He *owns* your husband –

(**MEG** *is confused.*)

Think Darwin.

MEG. Cynical.

AUROCH. Skeptical. I went to college, too. Well, grazed outside of one for a while. Ruminated.

(*beat*)

MEG. Have you ever felt it?

AUROCH. What?

MEG. You know, the…*impulse.*

AUROCH. Oh, *that.* Sure, once a year.

MEG. But where are your – ?

AUROCH. Calves? Why am I alone? I ask myself that all the time. I wanted to people the world with aurochs – each time, that's what I feel, inside, while I'm *doing it,* but… You can't control them, you know? The first time, I thought it was a fluke, but. One after the next. Maybe I lead by bad example, but. They all just…get lured to the other side. The lights through the windows at night, the smell of hay, grain, bedsheets –

(*pause*)

Can I smell your breath? Please?

(**MEG**, *awkward at first, lets her. Over the fence,* **AUROCH** *brings her nose near,* **MEG** *exhales gently. A tender moment.*)

AUROCH. Something sweet on it.

(*pause*)

What do you get out of it?

MEG. Out of what?

AUROCH. This "domestic" business?

(*Pause.* **MEG** *can't answer.*)

It can be lonely. Being the only one. Sometimes. I wonder: Why am I? Because I *believe* in it? Because I like that word, *wild*, how it feels? And why does everyone choose the other road? Can you tell me?

MEG. I…don't know. I – I mean, personally – I guess it's because I get to keep it all together. You know? My world, around me, intact.

AUROCH. You get to do all that?

MEG. I thought so. I used to… But honestly? I don't remember choosing.

(**AUROCH** *takes the yellowed old paper from* **MEG***'s hand.*)

AUROCH. (*reads*) "The book of Nature is written in the language of mathematics. Its symbols –

AUROCH & MEG. (*from memory*) "are triangles, circles and other geometric figures –

MEG. "– without which it is impossible to understand a single word, without which –

AUROCH. "– there is only a vain wandering through a dark labyrinth."

(*pause*)

Yours?

MEG. No, it's – Galileo. From – my thesis. Or – notes from it. My "thesis-I-never-wrote."

(*pause*)

AUROCH. It's not so vain.

MEG. What's not?

AUROCH. The wandering.

(**AUROCH** *turns, leaves the book on the fence. She puts her finger to her lips, in the gesture of a moo.*)

(**MEG** *lifts her finger to her own mouth, mirroring.*)

(**AUROCH** *exits. The sound of a single cow mooing rises, and becomes distant.*)

Scene Four

(The kitchen. **BEN** *sits at the table, going over the accounts. It's a clear, sunny day. A brand new radio plays, clearly. A Top 40 song ends.* * **MEG** *enters with a bag, something a grad student would pack in, from the '60s. She places it at the door.* **BEN** *doesn't see, or he doesn't look. A political commercial starts: "It's morning again in America!" She shuts off the radio.)*

BEN. Well, the accounts are looking up! All that rain caused a lot of damage, but if you account for the profit from the bulls that lived – he said we could keep that, even though he paid for them – then you figure –

MEG. Ben, you don't have to do that anymore.

BEN. Well, we might actually break even this year. What are you talking about?

MEG. It doesn't matter if we break even. We don't have to anymore.

BEN. Land's got to pay for itself.

MEG. Then let him take the money for the bulls.

BEN. Don't look a gift horse in the mouth.

(pause)

Oh – there's a letter from Jenny.

MEG. Oh. What does she say?

BEN. Acting workshop's going well –

MEG. Oh, good.

BEN. Likes the city…

MEG. That's my girl.

BEN. Glad she did it…but –

MEG. I'm so glad. I *knew* –

BEN. – it's not for her. She's switching majors. You'll never believe it. Agriculture! Isn't that great?

MEG. Oh, God.

---

*Please see Music Use Note on Page 3.

BEN. Wants to take up organic farming – like that'll ever pay. But…well, looks like she'll be back home after all! *Next* summer, let's –

MEG. Ben?

BEN. I could start a little corner of the north field for her, for some projects. She could raise some organic grain, we'll give her a couple of cows…

MEG. Look at me.

BEN. She'll have an edge over her classmates, that's for sure.

MEG. I'm not….Ben? I'm not – *content*, I'm not – the words sound strange, I –

BEN. You should be – for her.

MEG. I don't want to be, I –

BEN. It's what she wants. She tried the other thing, and she –

BEN & MEG. …chose.

MEG. *(a discovery)* She did, didn't she?

(pause)

Did you ever have dreams, Ben?

BEN. Yup, sure I did.

MEG. What were they?

BEN. Right here. You know that. This, the farm, you, everything. I found it. And I grabbed it.

MEG. Right here?

BEN. We're the lucky ones, Meg. How many people get to do that? You seen the receipt for that chicken wire we bought last month?

MEG. Ben, when you look at me, what do you see?

BEN. I don't know what you're talking about.

MEG. Look at me. Please.

BEN. I know what you look like.

MEG. Things change. I –

BEN. Yup, even steven.

*(**MEG** puts her bag on the table.)*

MEG. I've packed some things.

BEN. *(catches his breath)* I asked about the chicken wire.

MEG. Listen.

BEN. I didn't see anything, Meg. Consider it forgotten.

MEG. It's not him.

BEN. Matt needs his mom.

MEG. I'm not leaving Matt.

> (**BEN** *sighs a sharp, relieved breath.*)

I'm leaving this. I can't see it anymore, Ben.

BEN. *(with difficulty) I* need you.

MEG. Come with me. We can all go. Together. It's not too late. We're not so old.

BEN. Don't be ridiculous.

MEG. We have skills. We've got *his* money. We could –

BEN. You're making too much out of this. Look at that view. Beautiful. Nothing's changed – It's still there, I mean, *look*. I fell in love with that. That…those hills, that – when I first saw that, I knew, I wanted to wake up to that every day, see the sun move across her back… One hill, rolling into the next. Kind of muddy, but – it doesn't matter. That face, it's still her, it's still… so beautiful. Oh, look…I think you can, yep, there it is, look – Vermont.

MEG. – relocate, I was going to say. *We* could relocate.

(She looks out at everything, tries to see it, can't.)

Hills, grass, patches of brown; a couple barns, some rusty old equipment, a clothesline, a fence…What makes a home? A bunch of odd pieces, that you will together. People, things. That you make fit. It feels so strong, but…one sharp blow, and…it all seeps out. All that glue. All I can see are the pieces now. It's just –

(She turns to him.)

eyes lips nose…

(He keeps his eyes on the landscape.)

gone.

(pause)

Things change. You can only keep up the veneer for so long.

BEN. I can.

MEG. This isn't a contest.

BEN. Jesus Christ, Meg, work with me here. You think I like being weak? Biting my tongue? Being turned into a playground? But we can hang onto it, this way, don't you see? The joke's on him. He gets bored, he goes home, he will – I've seen his kind before. And then… it's ours again. He'll go and we'll be…the same. The same as we were before. You've just got to hold on a little, Meg, be a little weak, to get what you want.

MEG. My god, she's right. I really am.

BEN. What? Who?

MEG. A kept cow.

(beat)

BEN. Sweetheart?

(Lights begin to shift:)

MEG. Mmmm… mmmmm….

BEN. Are you okay? Honey?

(Interior: **MEG***)*

MEG. Mmmmooooooooooo.

(Her moo grows from tentative to strong, then reverberates as it unleashes a mythical element, a magical cacophony of distant mooing, jangling bells, a crash.)

(Beat. Lights return to normal.)

*(***MEG*** turns to leave.)*

BEN. Where will you go?

MEG. *(beaming)* I don't know. Out there.

(pause)

What's past Vermont?

(She goes to leave, pauses at the door. Looks back.)

(**BEN** *refuses to look; he keeps his eyes firmly on the land-scape.*)

(*She leaves.*)

(*He struggles to keep his eyes fixed; they flood with tears.*)

Scene Five

(In the semi-darkness, **MATT** *and* **VERONICA** *emerge. They stumble a little, because it's dark.* **MATT** *is in front, he holds her hand, to guide her.)*

MATT. Here, we're almost…ok. Here.

VERONICA. Here? We're in the middle of the field.

MATT. No, between fields. This – careful.

VERONICA. It's a wire.

MATT. A fence.

VERONICA. That'll do a lot. It's *wire.*

MATT. It's electric.

VERONICA. Oh –

(She jumps back.)

MATT. No, it's not that strong. It won't kill you. It – hurts, but not too much, not when you get used to it… It hurts, but you can take it.

(He puts out his hand, touches it, kicks his hand back. He reaches out again, closes his hand around the wire, counts 5, releases. Whenever one of them touches the fence, we hear its sound: a steady, electric ticking.)

You try.

VERONICA. It'll hurt.

MATT. Well, yeah. But then…it turns into something else.

(She touches it, jolts back.)

VERONICA. Ow.

MATT. You've got to keep your hand there.

(She does, a second.)

Again.

(She holds on this time. He has to pull her away.)

VERONICA. My god, it – it pulses.

MATT. That's the electricity. It comes in surges. It's from a car battery.

VERONICA. It felt like a heartbeat.

(beat)

MATT. Yeah.

(Final interior: alone, and together)

(They look at each other, take a breath, simultaneously reach out, and…grab the fence. They close their eyes. Ten-count, to the pulse of the fence.)

*(**BEN** sits in half-light, staring out at the landscape, tears streaming down his face.)*

*(**JAMES** leans into the belly of his cow.)*

*(**MEG** crosses through them to the gate. Touches it. It creaks open. She walks through the fence.)*

(A song plays: something like "Picture This" by Blondie.)*

(Lights.)

End of Play

---

* Please See Music Use Note on Page 3.

ABOUT THE PLAYWRIGHT

Emily DeVoti's plays have been presented in NYC by New Georges, Rattlestick Theater, New York Theater Workshop, ArsNova, Abingdon Theater, HotINK/NYU, Cherry Lane Theatre, Six Figures, Judith Shakespeare Company, Perry Street Theater and Rising Phoenix Rep; in London, by the Royal National Theatre and Out of Joint; regionally by Shakespeare & Co. (Lenox, MA). Her plays have been published by Samuel French, Inc. and Smith&Kraus and supported by residencies with The Orchard Project and The MacDowell Colony. She is a member of New Georges' Kitchen Cabinet and a founding editor and current Theater Editor of The Brooklyn Rail. She holds an MFA in dramatic writing from NYU/Tisch, where she was a Goldberg Award-winner, and an A.B. from Princeton University, where she won the Grace May Tilton Prize in Fine Arts. She has taught playwriting at NYU/Tisch and Mt. Holyoke College.

Other full-length plays include: *Dirt* (the drama of a cross-class, fetishistic love affair in Victorian London), *Meat* (a modern tale of a butcher, Hitler, and apartment grubbing in Brooklyn), *In Ipswich Waiting* (a counter-*Crucible* set during the witchcraft scares of 17th century New England), *Beyond the Veil* (a fictitious meeting between Edith Wharton and W.E.B. DuBois), *Marianne: A Revolution in 3 Acts* (the story of a Parisian seamstress and her political awakening amidst the rise and fall of the Paris Commune), and an adaptation of Henry James's *The Turn of the Screw.*

www.ingramcontent.com/pod-product-compliance
Lightning Source LLC
Chambersburg PA
CBHW070639120726
47909CB00004B/1498